ANGIE'S MOVE

The First Novel

by

Joshua Ramírez

Los Angeles, CA

Happy families are all alike;
every unhappy family is unhappy
in its own way.
--Leo Tolstoy, *Anna Karenina*

*When you're married, you'll understand the
importance of fresh produce.*
--Tony Soprano,"D-Girl"S2E7

THE PROLOGUE

A lot of people like to argue the opposite, but it's pretty obvious that sports bring people together more than they drive them apart. It would be shortsighted to look at the more intensive rivalries as the basis for believing that sports instill tribalism and xenophobia. It's true that you wouldn't make many friends in Boston while wearing New York baseball clothing, and if you already had animosity toward a person, knowing that their allegiance lies with the thorn in your favorite team's side could make it so that this animosity never faded. However, when it comes down to it, there are more opportunities where our love of a game, or many games, sparks connection and community. After all, nothing starts a conversation better than: "Did you see the game last night?"

In fact, it was a question close to this one that brought together Angela Saccomanno and Jackson Norossi. See, Jackson and Angela, although they had no idea at this point, shared one common and fateful interest: they were both major supporters of the Los Angeles Kings, a club in the National Hockey League.

Angela, usually partial to the shortening "Angie", was initially and primarily an Angels' fan, oddly enough, coming from baseball roots that included her father having been a top recruiting prospect for the Baltimore Orioles. Despite never knowing her father, with him removing himself from her life shortly after her birth, she still managed to inherit much of his athletic tendencies, and was always the stand-out in everything from a P.E. kickball game to the CIF-Southern Section Softball State Championship. Fast forward about a decade from that game and you would find her comfortably employed by the parent company of the Staples Center, where she would spend her days impressing executive after executive with her prowess for fan interaction and experience across the NBA, the WNBA, and of course, the NHL.

Jackson, similar to his Angie, liked his moniker to be shortened to "Jack". He had been a Kings' fan since birth--his father made sure of it, swaddling him in black and silver right out of the womb. However, unlike his love interest, he was not athletically inclined. Jack was more of a desk job type. He found his strengths in organization, project management, and professional networking. These talents eventually landed him a job as an account manager with a strong marketing firm on the westside, where he made himself a comfortable living that afforded him all the hockey games he pleased. Fortunately for him, his lifetime love of the game that he would refer to as Canada's greatest gift to the world would soon turn around and gift him perhaps the only thing he would ever love more than the thrill of a well-set up one-timer.

They met on a Thursday night, when the stadium is generally the least populated. The team was having by all accounts a bad season and as a result, attendance was down in general. This is important because it allowed less distraction and less margin for error in the moment that needed to take place. Jack and his older brother Paul arrived at the gate and quickly made their way to the secret beer cove to grab their first brew. (You had to be "in-the-know" to get to this place.) It was tucked right by the Figueroa entrance, but so direct that it often went unnoticed and thus had virtually no wait time. If you were fine drinking a canned domestic or the most basic of IPA's, this was the place to get your fix.

You also had to be "in-the-know" to avoid the salesmen that camp out by that area, waiting to prey on the excited, but so very naive hordes of Kings' faithful. The avoidance technique was as simple as hugging to the left part of the hallway, but this beer cove had a natural blind spot precisely because of its hidden location, so you always ran the high risk of slamming into somebody when taking this route. Jack had succeeded without contact in this maneuver very regularly, and fortunately, he never experienced anything worse than a slight bump and a nervous "oop" when running into someone also hugging that side of the wall in the opposite direction.

This held true until this very night.

Leading the way to the ice for warm-ups, Jack had a pep in his step as he cautiously made the left toward his section. It was right then that he all but high kneed a child's Coke and nachos right out of his hands. (Interesting how often fate resorts to this type of messy meddling.) After Jack made sure the kid was unharmed, he gave him some cash to replace the snacks and then made his way back to replace his own. However, his brother was kind enough to stop him before he got too far and pointed out the obvious cheese stain on his favorite Wayne Gretzky jersey. After a lightspeed value analysis, Jack decided to just forget the beer and head to the men's room, where he quickly soaked up the stain in hopes of still catching the players' entrance.

The brothers finally made their way to the ice and just managed to see their Kings fire out and start chucking pucks at the net. Of course, they couldn't get their normal place right up against the glass because of the delay and this upset Jack more than he let on, but he was mature enough to shake it off and enjoy himself nonetheless. However, he wasn't about to stand a row or two back from the glass in a pathetic attempt to get close "enough" to the action. Instead, he told his brother they should just watch from the top of the lower bowl. Paul agreed and they found satisfaction in just being able to watch any of the warm-ups at all after that early mishap.

The Norossi family were not much for talking, even though they had a reputation for being social and noticeably friendly. In fact, this was one allure of hockey as a family affair for them. The game is one of very distinct sounds, from the slap of the composite sticks on the ice, to the blades of the skates grinding up frozen showers to stop the behemoths piloting them, it's most definitely an auditory experience. Thus the brothers stood and took it all in without so much as a word between them.

These sounds persisted even as Jack's attention shifted from the visuals of the players to the caramel-haired woman in a business suit standing across the arena just above the highest row in the lower bowl. He didn't know it at the time, but this was Angela, the woman who would inspire enough nerves to make him puke monstrously just moments before presenting her with a ring and asking her to stand by his side until he couldn't stand anymore. At this time, all he knew was that he'd never seen such beautiful hair. Of course, he also didn't realize (and never would) that had he not laid out that child earlier in the evening and stained his favorite material possession in the process, he would not have been so far from the glass that he could have noticed this feature of his future lover.

Her long mane of sheeny brown hair was her genetic blessing bestowed upon her from her Abruzzo ancestors. The follicles cascaded over her petite shoulders, along her well-tailored suit all the way down to her lower back, creating a highly feminine and very encapsulating image. It was as he continued to study her beauty that his brother called his name and suggested they grab another beer before the game starts. Jack looked back down to the ice and noticed it was empty. He had completely missed the last ten minutes of warm-ups.

By the time the Kings fell down two goals, Jack decided he needed to stretch his legs and maybe check out the Team Store. Making his way down the hallway, he was surprised--though thinking back he couldn't tell you why--to see that Angie was alone, on her phone, right by his section. He managed to fight off the panic and started walking forward, hoping that her phone would sufficiently keep her attention and prevent her from looking up and seeing him--despite the fact that all he truly wanted at that moment was in fact, her attention. Jack kept his gaze forward, but his pupils remained on her as he crept forward at a slightly more hastened pace. Much to his horror, she looked up at him and although she met him with a smile, it faded almost immediately. Completely shook, he nearly sprinted past, retreating once more into the men's room.

Obviously unbeknownst to him, Angie's smile faded because of how scared Jack looked as he passed her. She was concerned about what would make a grown man feel such fear, completely unaware that it was her own beauty that had done it. She went back to her phone and continued pinning outfits for her non-existent toddler.

4

Meanwhile, Jack caught his breath and decided that enough time had passed for her to go back to her business and for him to safely head back to his seat. He was wrong. Upon making his way back to the hallway, Angie was still there, still buried in her phone. The choice from here was obvious, even though it wasn't ideal: enter through the other aisle and climb over thirty fans to get to his seat. Jack went ahead and braved the sneers and jeers, and found his space next to Paul.

During the second intermission, Paul suggested they grab one last beer and Jack made a poor attempt to dissuade him. See, Jack is not only shy, but he's a people pleaser. He is incapable of doing anything that serves himself. Paul is also a people pleaser, however he's less of one than his brother, so he won the battle. It goes without saying that Paul was not going to climb over 29 Kings' fans when they could just go through the Angie-guarded exit, but fortunately for Jack, Angie was no longer guarding the tunnel and they were able to head to the beer stand without interruption.

That girl with long hair was cute, huh?, Paul asked, shocking Jack.

Which one?

C'mon. The one you were staring at during warmies.

Jack had a nice olive hue, perhaps his best gift from his Sicilian ancestors, but he still managed to blush at the comment. His brother had always been good at reading him, often better than he was at reading his own damn self. However, this was no comfort because his overactive mind made him believe that Angie had also seen how flushed he was over her and was perhaps perturbed by it.

Oh, yeah. Haha. She was cute, he replied.

We should hang out right here after and see if she comes by.

We have like five minutes before the game's back.

It's 4-0.

Once more a victim to his people-pleaser tendencies, Jack relented and sipped on the fresh brew with his brother in the hallway, praying to any power greater than his that Angie wouldn't come strutting down that hallway. Fate, of course, wouldn't be so accommodating.

Angie came down the hallway not even five minutes into the final period of the game, and Paul immediately started hounding. The sound of her heels clacking violently against the linoleum was like needles in the shy man's eardrums, each CLACK driving the point deeper into the canal.

Go ahead. I'll watch your beer, Paul said as he started pulling the drink away from Jack's sweaty hands. *Just ask a stupid question like 'Where's the bathroom?' Just gotta get the ball in play, big dog.*

If Jack had a bit more of a spine, he would have scoffed at his brother's pressure or he might have even just went ahead and walked back to his seat of his own accord. Of course, he was on the lower percentile of self-assertion and thus had no recourse other than at the very least speaking to the breathtaking woman that was very quickly making her way right toward him.

It really was quite amazing how quickly she moved in slow motion. Angie was by all means a go-getter, perpetually rushing her friends and family enough to develop a reputation of being a rather harsh and anal person. This was so much so that other members of her inner circle often set times for events and departures that were separate for her, to avoid the intense dictatorship that might occur if they were even so much as five minutes off the agreed-upon time.

She hurried down the hallway in an effort to get back to her office as soon as possible so she could send her last emails of the night and get the hell out of Downtown. As would be expected, nearly any delay would have set her off at that high stress point in the night. Yet, when Jack approached her, she immediately softened. Angie is not a liar and she would never explicitly state that Jack's looks got her attention, but she is also not a superficial person. She would later say that his warm and gentle manner was the first thing she picked up from him in their initial meeting. It was a feeling inside her that no one had previously elicited and the ability this then-stranger had in calming her work-related anxiety was something she valued very much.

Excuse me. Do you work here? Jack asked.

Yes. Can I help you?

Do you work... for Staples Center, or the Kings, or something else?

Staples Center. I work with in-game entertainment. Are you looking for a job?

In a shock even to himself, the smile that she gave him after this quip did not weaken his knees to the point where he couldn't stand. The smile actually comforted him, much like how his manner alone had comforted Angie. He smiled back and to his blissful joy, her own grin grew wider.

Jack and his brother exited Staples Center and made their way to the train station without much to say to each other. Their team had been beaten so badly that they didn't even need to pull their goalie in a last ditch effort to remain competitive. They had just rolled over and died--no fight at all. Although he would have liked to see his team win, or at least not give up so pathetically, Jack took an extra bit of pleasure on the walk to the station with the knowledge that he himself had put up a much more successful fight in that arena this very night. He had talked to what he would come to confirm was the most beautiful woman in the world, and he had done a fine job of coming off as himself at his best.

Once seated in the car, the operator set forth on the rail toward their home stop. Paul finally leaned over and gave him a friendly ribbing. In true Norossi fashion, no words needed to be spoken. Jack had done it, and he knew very well that he wouldn't have done it without the help and incessant determination of his older brother. He spent the next six stops peering out the window at the quiet Los Angeles night, thinking to himself of how his life would change. Jack was a simple man for the most part, but he had definitely felt that Angela was different and that making that move toward getting to know her had not only signaled a personal evolution, but a full life shift.

Jack didn't know it then, but he would go on a date with Angela the following week after spending four full days staring at her phone number before he made the call to set up the meeting. Jack and Angie would have a great first few dates, then they would become exclusive and finally he would meet her mother and sisters, and she would meet the infamous Norossis. They would grow closer and closer, begin to take trips to Las Vegas, San Francisco, and even Mexico City. Finally, as they continued to fall deeper and deeper in love and with the aid of a few years of gestation, Jack would take that leap that every young man fears. Angie would push back tears, stick out her left hand, and vehemently accept his proposal.

Young love is a special kind of foolishness. It should be clear that the term "foolishness" is not one that equates to stupidity or anything as negative a term like that. This foolishness is not because lovers can be blinded by their passion, or because their youth does not afford them the necessary life experience. It comes from their ability to place high stakes on something as fickle as attraction. Love, like any relationship, must be built over time. This doesn't mean the three to five years that has become standard, at least in American marriages. Ask a long time friend. If you have been fortunate enough to have a friendship that has lasted at least a decade, you can more than likely recall many good times and many bad times. However, if you are still friends, you can also reflect on how little the bad times mattered in the long run. Think again about friendships that fizzled. There must have come a point in those relationships where one party realized that the partnership was not worth upkeeping and there is certainly no shame or blame in making that decision.

Yes, love is an action-oriented affair and like a muscle, it must be exercised and exerted regularly to grow stronger. The same principle applies to family. We love our families because they are our blood, true, but the greater factor is that we simply have known them for our whole lives, or their whole lives. We've seen our siblings become adults, our parents become elders, and our elders meet their deaths. There have been major turning points in our lives where we needed our family's support, and if we were lucky, we got it. There are no real ups and downs with family, because they're family and we cannot really break from them in any normal circumstance.

Marriage, for lack of a better word, marries these concepts together. We take a person that we fell in love with and we make them family. They have holiday dinners with our parents. We start to hug their great aunts. Eventually their siblings' children become our nieces and nephews. However, these lines can never be wiped clear, they can only be blurred, at least in the beginning. Time is the missing ingredient and it must be used generously. This, of course, is much more difficult than it may sound because time is not neutral. During this time will come trials and tribulations that will shake and dismantle even the strongest of partnerships. The muscles of a couple's love will need to be enduring and prepared for a challenge at any moment. The weights of money, trust, support, and endless other life exercises threaten to strain those muscles and even tear them in places that will render them useless. There must be a mix of luck, dedication, and desire to the partnership and the love between them that both must believe can never be replicated.

When Jack and Angie informed their respective loved ones of their choice to love each other exclusively, they were instantly met with the expected hugs and cheers. These Norossi and Saccomanno supporters had been there for Jack and Angie through thick and thin and it went without saying that each one would sooner take a needle to the eye before seeing any harm befall their kin. In every way, that life-changing decision was as much a moment of change for them as it was for the couple. Truly, when Angie's lips met Jack's for the first time with that pure tint of love on each lip, the lines between lovers and family were officially blurred and just like that, the Norossi brothers had gained their first sister.

This is the story of that new family, but more importantly about how Angela Norossi affected the unit that had been galvanized to near-unbreakable levels over the years and years of maturation. Jack knew on that day that he would spend the rest of his life with this woman, and Angie, at least on some level, felt the same. What both had skipped over, however, was that when you promise your life to another, you can never give only that. No, you must give your family, and your family must accept the new addition as well. Family, after all, will always have been there for you longer.

MOVE-IN DAY

Those who have never lived in Southern California often have an inaccurate image and understanding of the territory. Even if one has paid a visit--assuming one ventured beyond the beaches, Hollywood Boulevard, and downtown--one would miss out on so much of this particular part of the world. There is simply no possibility that anyone other than a true native can understand all that goes into a life that borders Mexico, the Pacific Ocean, Nevada, Arizona, and sadly, Northern California.

Both Jack and Angie could boast such a life with the former growing up in the Inland Empire and the latter in East Los Angeles. Although the localities were very different, it was something they shared in common and shared understandings like these are so often the base of strong relationships. This couple was no exception as they often went out together to one's favorite bar, restaurant, and cafe only to discover that the other partner was also a regular patron of the same spot. These even extended beyond Southern California, such as lesser-known stops on and off the Las Vegas Strip, all the way to must-see points in Oakland, and even hidden gems in New York City. In fact, when they had finally decided to move in together, they had to have many discussions about where they would choose to spend these next impactful moments, and not all of these places were in their home state.

At this time, Jack was currently living with two of his brothers and his cousin in a two-bedroom apartment in the Inland Empire, while Angie lived with a roommate in the South Bay. Fortunately, both earned respectable salaries and their options were for the most part open to their liking. They had initially discussed moving Jack in with Angie, and asking her roommate if she would be so kind to relinquish her residency in a timely manner out of respect to the couple. Angie was not too sure how this would be received, but their relationship was strong enough that she was willing at least to bring it up. This made the most sense right away because Angie's living quarters were nicer, had a better location, and it would be gentlemanly for Jack to allow her to avoid the hassle of moving--not to mention that it would be awkward if the couple had to

13

live with additional roommates. Of course in addition to that distaste, there was the added obstacle of Jack having to ask one of not only his roommates, but family members to abdicate the room they shared, or the apartment altogether. Jack was certain this would be problematic, because unknown to Angie, he covered the majority of living expenses for some of his cohabitants on a semi-regular basis. Thus, no one in that apartment outside of Jack could afford to move. In fact, even if Jack was the only one to leave, there would be problems.

After further discussions, the two decided that since both earned comfortable livings and they were most definitely in love and in this for the long haul (even though Jack had yet to propose--more on that later), that they should look for a property of their own in lieu of an apartment. They searched high and low across the Southland for a spot that both would enjoy in terms of locale and one that would prove to be a smart investment in this challenging market. Soon enough, they came upon a quaint home in the San Gabriel Valley, just west of Jack's quarters, that proved to be affordable, was seated in a fantastic neighborhood, and would have enough space in the case of additions to their family unit. They were so convinced upon the tour that it took less than a day of discussion for them to decide and inform the agent that they were ready to make their offer. Not too long after that phone call, the home was theirs.

The 2,000 square foot/four bedroom/two bathroom house was nestled right in the center of the block on a street more busy than they would have liked, but this was their home now and they loved even the less than desirable elements all the same.

Spring had just begun and the couple stood in front of their new home on this sunny afternoon, just appreciating the curbside appeal for a moment. They were about a month from their move-in date and had a lot of planning to do before then. For now, they forgot about all of that and instead focused on the future and all the abundance that it held--a large majority of which would occur inside those very walls.

Jack thought to himself about how lucky he had been these past few years. Not only to find Angie, secure her affection, then discover she was at the exact point in her life where she was ready for him, but with his recent career advancements and bumps in salary, he was finally ready to buy his own home and take yet another giant step toward true adulthood. In an almost ridiculous addition to his good fortune, Angie had agreed to allow his brother Raphael to move in with them. This had been bothering Jack for some time. He knew it would be a lot to ask Angie to let his brothers come with him, but he also knew that his brothers wouldn't take the news of his departure well. In what would most certainly not be the last time, he was stuck between pleasing his life partner and pleasing his blood.

As was expected, both Raphael and the younger Isaac were not happy with the news. Isaac obscenely asked if Jack was joking and then added to it by asking him what they were supposed to do now. Raphael--known by the brothers as *Snacks* both for his conspicuous paunch and because he could often be heard chomping on something or other at all hours of the day--shook his head and expressed how he couldn't believe Angie was already bossing him around when they weren't even married yet. Jack was at least spared his cousin Bart's anger. He took the news much better and came to the conclusion that he should move in with his longtime girlfriend, too, which he had been putting off, much to her chagrin.

Jack tried to quell the tense situation by telling his brothers that the new home had four bedrooms and it was entirely possible that they could stay there in the meantime, as they looked for a new place to live. The last thing he wanted to do was to spring this on them and force them to go back to their mom and dad's house, especially since Isaac was currently unemployed and would be completely assed-out by the change. Snacks immediately jumped in and claimed that it was Isaac's fault he lost his job because of his own damn negligence and it was himself who should be given preference since he was the one who found this very apartment in the first place. Jack then reiterated that both would

15

potentially be invited to stay at their home in the transition as there were over two excess bedrooms and that he would never pick one brother over the other. Snacks was quick to confirm that statement before adding that fraternal preference was no issue since Jack had already picked Angie over all of his family.

Needless to say, this was not going well. Jack was actually happy when his brothers both retreated to their rooms in a fury and with a final slam of the doors, he had been released from the moment. He only hoped that the discussion with Angie would be better.

Under the cool Las Vegas desert air, the couple made their way toward the Cosmopolitan for a weekend in one of their favorite getaways. Jack was clever enough to know that his request would be that much easier when Angie was relaxed in her favorite Vegas bar, preferably after adding a few extra dollars to her account after a pleasant night at the Blackjack tables.

Lady Luck was very much with the young man that weekend and this exact moment actually did occur. Angie had found a hot shoe at the $25-limit game at Caesar's Palace and rode it to over $1,000 in profits. Being a vivacious and boisterous woman by nature, she exploded with exuberance any time she hit a gambling hot streak. She was dancing along the casino carpet, hugging and kissing her future house mate, and sharing the details of their new home with any stranger who would listen. Jack found so much beauty in Angie when she was like this. Her energy was one of his favorite things about her, and her Vegas energy was on a completely different level. However, this did not do much to help his cause, because he shuddered at the thought of squashing this outburst of joy by presenting her with an unfavorable living situation in a home that she was so thrilled to occupy. Jack decided his only course of action was to head right to The Chandelier, her all-time favorite watering hole, and let her imbibe to her heart's content, then present her with his potential arrangement.

It took about three exotic fruit-infused cocktails for Angie to become a broken record for how much she loved Jack, and how lucky she felt sitting across from him right now. Jack figured there'd be no better time to ask that question that had been churning his guts for weeks, so he went ahead and began the pitch.

You make Vegas so much fun, he began and after which he was immediately granted a long, albeit sloppy kiss.

I never knew Vegas until I met you. I'd been to all the clubs, all the bars, all the casinos, parties, whatever. Then I came once with you and was like, FUCK that. This... this is Vegas, she expressed before dropping her throbbing head on his chest.

Jack waited a moment to let her calm down before he added how excited he was to move in with her. She agreed and said how nice it would be to come home to each other every single night.

I've been thinking. Maybe I'm just being paranoid, but since I'll still be working in Highland Park, there's going to be times when I don't get home until pretty late. You're going to be in that big house by yourself, Jack relayed.

Don't scare me like that! Angie snapped as she whacked her boyfriend in his chest. *I never even thought of that, but who cares. I'll get a gun--a big one.* Her worry dissipated as she laid her head back on Jack, whose own worry was growing with every passing moment. This was happening so quickly that he came to the conclusion that he needed to just flat ask. No more building to the punch or taxing set-ups, he needed to present his thoughts and they can discuss them like adults.

I only brought it up because, as you know, my brothers are going to need to find someone to replace me, and actually, they'll need to find two because Bart is actually going to be moving in with Taylor soon. Honestly, I don't think they'll be able to find two people in time and they don't have the money to cover.

Is Isaac still looking for work? she responded without opening her eyes.

Yeah. It's getting close to the busy season so he'll find something soon, but he just can't make rent until then. Of course, I'm just going to end up loaning both of them the money to cover, and it would just be cheaper to have them live with us, like just for practicality.

Why would you end up loaning them the money? You should probably just tell them to figure it out. Snacks is like twenty years older than you and Isaac acts like he's fourteen. After a long yawn, she added, *Maybe they need a little adversity.*

Feeling the conversation not going exactly how he planned, Jack's worry became more pronounced and he nervously cleared his tightening throat. Angie sensed this and lifted her head, drunkenly staring at him for an exceedingly extended moment before asking, *Did you already tell them they could move in?*

Jack quickly denied it and instead made a point of how he was just thinking it made sense. He couldn't leave his brothers hanging after all.

A rapidly sobering Angie replied that he most definitely could, but if he already told them, then she wouldn't be opposed to a very, very short term during which Snacks would pay a fair rent and be responsible for his part of the house's upkeep. This relieved Jack immensely for a brief moment before she added that Isaac couldn't move in unless he was employed at the time of occupancy. She clarified that she didn't care if it was fast food or holding a sign in front of a mattress dealer, but no one was going to live in their house without an income--that would just be asking for problems. In a major power move that Jack by now was very much used to, she stood up, said that they should head back to the room, and began setting up the payment for the drinks.

Jack decided this was a fair compromise and when they got home from Vegas, he went right to Snacks and told him his good news, of course leaving out most of the conditions involved. When it came to Isaac however, he found it better to enlist Snacks' help in breaking that news. This did not work entirely how Jack thought, as Isaac immediately complained to him when he was told of the employment condition and began making his case for empathy by really hitting the subject of how he'd now be the only one in the apartment and it was only a matter of time before he ended up on the street. How could it possibly make sense to leave the unemployed tenant with the full rent? Snacks stood up for Angie right then by telling Isaac that it's their house and they can do what they want, which of course started a bigger argument between the brother who would be allowed to live there and the forgotten one. This argument boiled over and Isaac finally claimed that he was just going to live on some friend's couch. He refused to be a part of this household where he had no rights and the homeowners could make any rules they wanted, any time they wanted. Jack tried to calm him down, but he had no luck. Once again, their conversation ended with a door slam, although one less than before.

In the living room, Snacks consoled Jack by telling him that he gave them a fair deal and he didn't need to explain his decisions to anyone, even his brothers. He assured Jack that Isaac would cool down. He'd get to live with his buddy, find a new job, and everything will go back to normal. This is just a transition for all of them and those who were less prepared for it are suffering the most. He ended his talk by reminding Jack that he was not Isaac's father, and on top of that, Isaac is a grown man. His problems are his own. Jack agreed and took a deep breath. He thanked Snacks for being so mature about all of this, and told him that he was actually really glad that he'd be moving in with them in the new house. He would need his older brother's expertise in things like household maintenance and it would be great to have him at the house so Angie isn't alone too often.

It's gonna be a perfect fit, Snacks added with a comforting pat on the shoulder. *Guess I better start packing.*

The day finally came when Jack, Angie… and Snacks moved into their dream home. It was a Saturday morning, far later than Angie had planned. She walked around Jack and Snacks' apartment trying to fathom a world in which it would have made sense for them to leave so

19

many things unpacked until moving morning. Being the efficient worker that she is, Angie instead pushed those thoughts and judgments to the side and focused on throwing the majority of Jack's things into whatever boxes were available and getting him to load the van instead of spending all his time picking which songs he should play during the move

She did not even want to look in Snacks' room--for many reasons--but she could only imagine what kind of mess laid within, and just how many things that he had yet to pack. In fact, at this point, she didn't even know where he was at. Jack didn't know either and she started to worry that he wasn't even here. Right as she was about to break down and enter Snacks' room, she heard a knock on the door. It was the property manager who was rightfully upset that it was already thirty minutes past the agreed-upon exit, and the apartment looked in no shape to be inspected.

I know. I'm sorry. I'm trying to get these boys to hurry. I don't understand why they're not packed, either, she tried to laugh off, but received no sympathy from the already-sour man. *I'm very sorry, two of the tenants are completely moved out, so if you'd like to start with those rooms and their bathroom, please go right ahead.*

The peeved man did not find the compromise appealing and told her that he would be back in thirty minutes, after which he would be forced to charge them for an extra weekend of rent. Angie apologized once more and went right to Jack.

Can you please call Snacks? The manager just told me he's going to charge you guys for an extra weekend. And what are we supposed to do with the junk Bart and Isaac left? Do they even care about getting the deposit back?

Well... probably not, because I paid it, he replied.

Angie took a deep breath and grit her teeth to push the stress as far away from her as possible. She instead turned her focus to their beautiful home and all the much better memories that the two of them would create because of it and inside of it. She calmly told Jack to pack up all his shit ASAP and how it was in his best interest to get Snacks here right now and for the two of them to get the van loaded in any way possible so they can get the hell out of here before she ruins her $50 manicure by grabbing both of them by their fat throats and choking them within an inch of their lives. Jack agreed and got to work wrangling Snacks, who had actually went out to get a quick breakfast. Why he didn't ask anyone if they wanted something, much less inform them that he was leaving was anybody's guess.

Thirty minutes later, the van was loaded, the landlord had completed his exit inspection, and the trio were all set to head out. Angie went ahead and recapped the next phase of the move to the brothers since they apparently needed extra attention when it came to these matters. After asking them if they understood, and receiving confirmation, she handed the keys to the moving van to Snacks, who kept his arms firmly down to signal his rejection.

What are you doing? she asked while using all of her available strength to not hock the keys right between his sleepy eyes.

Didn't Jack tell you? I got my license suspended.

When did this happen?

Two weeks ago. I got pulled over and my insurance lapsed. I was gonna pay it after the move because I wasn't sure if we needed to pay any rent for the upcoming month. Anyway, I can't drive for like sixty days or something.

I asked you Thursday and you said you'd drive the van, she half-screamed.

Oh, I thought you meant like load the van. I was gonna just load and unload since I couldn't drive.

You didn't even load it!

The outburst froze both brothers and she quickly realized just how intensely she had snapped at him. She collected herself and calmly asked Jack to drive instead. She would happily take Jack's car and give Snacks a ride. Jack replied with what she absolutely did not want to hear: that Snacks' car is still here so they need to take a few trips to get all three vehicles to the house. Jack had thought they would take Angie's car first, then quickly head back with her to get his car, and finally make the trip one more time to get Snacks' car, and during those excursions Snacks would hopefully finish unloading the van.

Angie paused for a beat, trying her hardest not to scream once more. This had obviously been a plan they had conceived without ever consulting her and then they didn't even have the decency to inform her until right at this very moment. She almost did not even want to ask: *And why can't you drive the van?*

I don't know how to drive those things, responded the man with whom she was sure she would one day conceive children.

With her stress having whittled the fight in her down to nothing, she agreed to their plan. She hopped into the moving van without another word and headed down the street to the onramp, trying to remain grateful for her new home and praying that these two would break out of this communication deficiency at least for the duration of this move. Driving along the jammed freeway, she breathed slowly and comforted herself by thinking how the hardest part of the transition was removing them from their apartment, and now that it was over, she could at the very least handle the rest of the problems on her literal home turf.

She really did love this house, and she must have really really loved Jack, because she could already feel that she was making massive compromises that she had not planned on needing. In fact, she couldn't even remember a time previous to this where she had to alter one of her fool-proof plans so damn much. Mostly a function of the extended drive that dragged and dragged along the god-awful 10 freeway, she came to find that this line of mishaps had actually been a very good thing. She was growing as a person and learning how to be more adaptable to the many curveballs of life. She had a plan. It was botched. She adapted, and they still achieved the same goal. In truth, she had to thank Jack and his brother for this unexpected benefit. As she exited the freeway and made the turns toward their street, she was very much looking forward to the many personal augmentations these two Norossi boys would bring about in her in the near future.

...

Angela Saccomanno was not born tough, but she was given the opportunity to grow into the fierce woman that she is today almost immediately. She entered this world via Liam and Amanda Gualtieri as the youngest of three sisters, Berenice and Charlotte having arrived earlier. Much like the other three girls, she grew very attached to their kind, loving, but very strict mother. This became a necessity when at just two years old, her feckless father resigned from his duties and left the four women to fend for themselves without so much as a note. Although a traumatic event, no doubt, it was this selfish act of the man who gave her life that made her and her family unit the galvanized one they are today. In fact, it did not take long for Angie's mother to revert back to her maiden moniker, Saccomanno, and as an act of unity, all the daughters followed suit.

As the baby of the family, Angie was bequeathed the benefit of seeing both of her sisters' mistakes and learning from them without personal consequences. She was wise enough to use this advantage often and thus was immune to many of the harsher lessons of life, which moved her along the ranks of school, sports, and relationships much quicker, but with the cost of a deep-seated naivete. Unfortunately, this could best be seen when the stakes were the highest. To give an example, she would select classes in high school with the consultation of her sisters who could recommend the most lenient teachers and the best ways to secure a top grade. Angie would, of course, finish with a stunning GPA, but she knew well that both her SAT and AP scores suffered substantially from the lack of actual understanding of the material. This all culminated in her missing out on all of her top school choices, but her determination only grew with the failures and she had both the work ethic and dedication to get the most out of any situation thrown at her.

23

Upon the completion of her undergraduate studies, Angie took a job at a law firm where she assisted paralegals with a wide range of cases. She had no interest in legal work, but she figured it would be wise to get some professional experience while she saved up for her Masters' course work, which she was set to start as soon as financially appropriate. The job was of course excruciatingly boring and she was barely compensated for her effort when you factored in the high rates this particular firm charged. (They even made her pay for parking, at their own building.) Although she became friendly with a horde of top attorneys from whom she would receive numerous invaluable letters of recommendation, her prime takeaway from that job was simply that she would do anything she could from that point on not to get stuck in an office like that.

True to her word, she began working as a customer relations specialist at a local venue soon after. Here, Angie really found her calling, with the loud music at night, the hip, interesting clients, and of course, the free and ever changing hours. It was while working here that she completed the majority of her dating. Being an attractive woman with a personality many eligible bachelors would describe as 'spitfire', she had no shortage of offers. In fact, she used to joke--never with Jack, of course--that she could have probably eaten every meal without spending a dime those few years. Angie went through the typical musician, businessman, model, and even dork, until the disillusionment began to set in and creeping thoughts common with women in their mid-twenties of dying childless and alone took firm root in her mind. Thankfully, she was raised right and knew her worth, so she continued to date top tier prospects with a healthy frequency, although this time around she was much more strict with who earned a second opportunity at her company.

Unfortunately, nothing stuck and she could not figure out why. She was not a particularly romantic person, but she did suffer from the typical beautiful young woman's desire to marry a rich, tall, and handsome man with a sparkling personality, lightning wit, and the incessant desire to write poetry and prepare romantic getaways in his free time. However, she was smart enough to know this man did not exist and whatever it was she was looking for would not arrive in the packaging she expected.

Meanwhile, her oldest sister, Berenice (better known as Bee), had just married a wildly successful entrepreneur. This wedding was a magnificent occasion for which their mother spared absolutely no expense (from his massive earnings). Angie loved the organizational elements and the many little traditions that went into preparing for such a big day and she loved the actual day even more. There was indeed a sort of malaise that fell upon her as the reception wound down and she realized that everyone was growing up and she had not even had a serious boyfriend yet. If she looked back now, she would find it ludicrous, but at that moment she felt as if everyone was so far ahead of her and her window to secure that perfect life, balanced with career, family, love, and happiness was just starting to close on her.

Angie ignored the noise and simply kept working harder at her job. Soon enough, she rose through the ranks to the booking department, where she began to increase her earnings exponentially while also garnering attention from top employers around the Los Angeles area in the process. She took lunches with executives and directors for much bigger companies, but was wise enough to wait for the perfect move to make her leap. This would come in about three months from that moment, when Staples Center came calling.

Not even six months into this new role, she received a phone call from her mother. Since it was on company time, she dismissed it, but three subsequent tries later, she finally answered. Battling tears, her mother informed Angie that she was going to be an aunt. Charlotte, the middle child, was welcoming the first grandchild for Mama Saccomanno this coming spring. Angie herself almost screamed at the news, jumping up and down with excitement. After ending the call, she ran through the office telling her co-workers how she was set to be "Auntie Angie".

It was only a few years later when she would walk along the hallways of Staples Center while the Kings were getting obliterated by the Florida Panthers, and a very shy, but even sweeter man by the name of Jackson would begin the process of stealing her heart. This would once more prove the value of patience, and reward Angela for consistently adhering to her high standards. She refused to marry the flashy club promoters. She turned down the tempting entertainment jobs offered to her. She even passed on a chance to become a regional manager for Enterprise Rent-A-Car. Angie always knew what she wanted and she had no fear in working or waiting for that perfect opportunity, but she also knew how to adjust her goals based on each particular situation. All of this maturity and focus led her to the unrivaled career position she currently held and to the partnership with the one-in-a-million Jack Norossi. She could now fall asleep next to him in their beautiful San Gabriel Valley home and express her gratitude for all that life had given her and all that it still had to give.

•••

A fundamental principle that both Jack and Angie thought they learned at an early point in life was that each person is always on their own timeline. There are endless factors when it comes to maturing, achieving life milestones, and building whatever they deem as a balanced existence. Just for some examples: Angie would be the last of her sisters to get married and Jack would be quick to avoid the subject of when exactly he lost his virginity. However, both tried to spend as little time as possible dwelling on the speed at which they reached these moments, because they understood that the timing was perfect for them and that was all that really mattered.

Snacks' timing was apparently just as unique, much to Angie's chagrin. It had now been over six months since they had moved in and

26

he still had some of his unopened boxes stacked in the corner of the living room.

Things had settled down from that hectic move-in day and the routine of actually living with one another had for the most part set in for the couple. Angie was comfortable cooking in her kitchen. Jack was elated to finally enjoy late nights of Simpsons' reruns on a TV where no one would bully him to change the channel. All was running smoothly as the shiny coat of novelty began to lose its shimmer in place of a warm layer of comfort and stability. To be honest, the two were even getting used to Snacks being there all the time, although this was mostly because he was very good at keeping to himself.

The only pressing issue at the moment was his boxes.

Mess in general annoyed Angie, but these boxes didn't perturb because of the sight or inconvenience of clutter. She just hated the concept that a grown man was able to see that disruption, know it was his fault, then continue to go about his day--filled with free time--and be perfectly content knowing his junk was ruining a public space. At this point in her naivete, she failed to realize that all of this extensive thought into what must go on in a grown man's head to allow boxes of his junk to just sit in the public living quarters... was completely for naught. Snacks didn't think one moment about the boxes. It was of no concern to him. So as Angie drove herself insane trying to gain his perspective, she missed the biggest personality point of Snacks, which was that to truly empathize with him, you simply had to think what would be the least amount of effort required to survive, and that's the path he would pursue.

See, Snacks was not a complicated man. He was fascinating to observe, true, but only because of how little he thought about his decisions. This ranged from boring routines like washing dishes all the way to massive life choices like if he should take a promotion offer at work. The best way to put it would be to think of how gurus are always telling people to: 'Live in the moment' and to 'Live every day as if it were your last'. Snacks must have heard this at an early age and locked in from there. He never left 'the moment'. The man would simply think

27

to himself, 'Would I replace the toilet paper roll if I knew I would die tonight? Of course not,' and the chore fell upon the next person.

Interestingly enough, the still honeymooning Angie would fail to see how her own lover displayed shades of these same traits. After all, Jack didn't unpack his things. Angie did. Maybe she realized this contradiction on at least a subconscious level and this was why she was reluctant to confront him about it. However, it was now about time to start entertaining--a big part of why they chose this particular house--and it was becoming more and more clear that Snacks was not going to clean his mess of his own accord. Angie even considered just throwing the boxes away. Whatever was in there obviously was not that important and if he was angry at the act, she could just say it was an accident. This line of thinking lost its allure as she realized that this was a short-term solution that would run the risk of begetting much bigger problems in the future, and she was not naive enough to fool herself into thinking Snacks was moving out anytime soon, so she decided it was better to just approach him amicably and ask him to move his shit as soon as he could accommodate.

Snacks somehow had been able to hold down a full-time job despite his inability to execute basic adult tasks. He was an assistant manager at a nearby Best Buy--the same Best Buy where he was hired about 15 years ago. He had managed to coast there for a good ten years before his superior told him that although his performance was decent, he was simply becoming too seasoned for this entry-level position. Performance review after performance review, Snacks had skillfully avoided a promotion in favor of the low-paid, but dead-easy position of working the register and stocking the shelves. The time had come for him to make a choice: accept the promotion or receive his notice. Snacks relented and accepted his new position as assistant manager and has since held this post.

His work hours were pretty regular, which made it all the more frustrating when Angie found it impossible to find him and then press him about moving his damn boxes. Angie spent the first five weeknights doing all of her leisure activities in the front room, expecting him to emerge at least to use the restroom at some point, but even pushing herself to stay up well past 23:00, he remained elusive. She was opposed to knocking on his door or even just sending him a text message because she didn't want him to think that she was being excessively naggy or god forbid, domineering. She felt that the three of them should all adopt an equal partnership in the home, even if all decisions would officially come down to the mortgagers' ruling. In her opinion, there was no need for a traditional hierarchy, and though she might not admit it, she would also have been hesitant to instill one due to the newness of their relationship and the overall situation. Her mention of the issue needed to come up as organically as possible and as if it weren't a big deal at all, which was becoming less and less true with each passing day.

Despite a heavy desire to believe otherwise, she was starting to feel like she was being avoided. Especially after she flaked on plans for that weekend specifically to run into him and he never showed. She had to really work hard to suppress these suspicions when she was sure he heard him run full speed to his car upon opening his bedroom door. She had shot out, too, but the sneaky tenant had beaten her out the front door, revved his engine, and sped off out of sight before she could get a word in.

Was he seriously avoiding her to get out of moving those boxes? Or was he hiding something even bigger from her? She confirmed that she needed to reach him post haste or else her paranoia would spike and this minor inconvenience would turn into a hurricane that would leave her undone and, of course, him no worse for it.

That next night she knew Snacks was going to be heading out with Jack to a concert and that they were scheduled to leave the house at 18:00. Determined to catch her prey, Angie literally sat in front of his door, leaning her back against the wood until he emerged. She had her earphones in, her favorite LA Kings' podcast playing, and she even had a broom right next to her, too, so she could act like she just happened to be

29

sweeping at the time. Of course, he opened it not even forty-five seconds into her sojourn and she had to get herself to her feet and laugh off the embarrassment of being caught lying in wait for him.

Hey, Snacks!

You okay? he asked as he gave her a mixed look of confusion and disgust that kindled her cheeks red with shameful heat.

Yeah, I was sweeping and thought I saw something on your door— anyway... are you going to the concert?

Uh huh.

Cool, I love that venue. You know, I almost got a job working with them. I interviewed and everything, and I was this close to accepting because I really liked where they were going. Like, tonight actually. 'Acute Cuneiform' is such a great fit, drum-heavy bands in those acoustics. Amazing. And every seat's a good one, Angie said as she resisted the urge to brush off the dirt on her pants that clearly proved she had not been sweeping.

Yeah, I've been there a few times. I'm sure AC'll kick ass in that set up, he replied.

For sure... Angie said as she stood blocking his path, panicking under the pressure of now having to actually confront him. *So... by the way, I'm glad I caught you,* she said as she forced some contrived laughter, *because I was gonna ask if you needed those boxes...*

In the living room?

Yeah, those. They've been in there and I'm like 'Did he forget that's his stuff?' The nerve-inspired laughter was enough to make Snacks visibly cringe as she continued, *I don't know. Just want to be sure in case they get tossed in the trash or even damaged. You know your brother. He might like knock them over or something. I just don't want anything to break, you know?*

Yeah, I'll get 'em. It's nothing important. I've just been putting it off, but I'll take care of it.

Awesome. Thanks, man, she said as she playfully punched him on the arm. *I don't know about you, but Jack and I are really having fun living here. Crazy how perfect it's been, huh?*

I never doubted it would be, he said in a tone that Angie initially read as offensive, until he added: *Thanks again for letting me stay here. Saved my ass big time.*

Oh, don't even mention it. We couldn't survive without you! Anyway, I'll let you go and get to the fun. Thanks again!

Angie turned to her bedroom and did her best not to rush out so she could take a huge breath of relief. She plopped onto her bed as she heard her boyfriend and his brother exit the house. She had done it. She got Snacks to acknowledge his mess and commit to righting the ship. Of course, she would have to stay on him until the boxes were officially unpacked, or at least moved into his room, but it was a good first step. Good enough in fact, that she felt she had well earned herself some ice cream and an hour of some garbage network TV binging.

One night after a particularly long week, Angela lied in bed with Jack as he flipped through the news channels, trying to find the one that shared his particular bias on a current event. She hated the news with a passion and instead dove into her copy of *Ulysses*, of which she made a habit of reading two pages every night. Finishing the last sentence of the page, she nodded to help convince herself that she had a handle on what was actually going on in that confusing orgy of literary grandeur. It was a warm night, so they left their bedroom door open, as well as the screen facing the backyard. This was important because it meant their conversation would echo down the hallway and if Snacks was so inclined, he could eavesdrop as he pleased--not that they would say anything negative behind his back, but still.

Angie leaned over to Jack and dove right in: *What was Snacks like as a kid?*

Jack replied without much vigor, *He was mom's favorite. Everyone says so.*

Really? It was that obvious? Feel like she showers you all with a ton of attention, but maybe it's because my mom wasn't super lovey dovey like that.

Yeah, she always served his meals first. You know how Italians are. Well, I guess you didn't have brothers, so maybe not. The oldest gets everything. Plus, he looked just like my mom's dad, which she mentioned like every day. She used to grab his face and squeeze it, saying 'Papa. Papa.' Isaac used to give him shit all the time for it, but it was obvious he was just jealous.

She processed this thought for a beat, then followed with: *Did she ever like outright favor him over your other brothers?*

It wasn't like she ever left us out. He just got his things first most of the time. One time when we were at our cousin's birthday party--I was eight; Snacks was fifteen, maybe he already turned sixteen. He's already a young adult or whatever, and I'm a little kid. Anyway, my aunt's cutting the cake and my mom's helping to hand out the slices to all the kids. Of course, Snacks gets his slice first. Not just before me, like she literally hands him a slice before my cousin, the birthday boy. In fact, she gave us all a slice before he got his. My aunt never forgot that, either. So, Snacks gets his slice first. He inhales it because it's his favorite flavor, and he immediately starts pestering my mom that he wants to go home. He's bored because it's all little kids and he wants to read comic books or whatever. Well, he bugs her enough that she packs us all into the car, my dad included, and half of us are like riding with a slice of cake in our laps, because we didn't finish eating and our aunt served everything on her nice plates that we couldn't take home. The worst part was me and my cousin were in the middle of planning the sleepover, which was now a no-go. It's dumb, but I guess I do think about it a lot.

Wow, Angie said as she began to put the puzzle together, *so did he wield that power? Or he just rolled with it?*

I wouldn't say he used it to his advantage necessarily. He knew he could get out of anything, but it's not like he weaponized that. I don't know, to be honest, we all knew how to butter up my mom. Like you said, she was always going to do anything for us.

That's sweet. She rested her head on his chest, happy to hear more and more about his family and upbringing, and getting a better perspective on Snacks was the icing on the cake. When talking with Jack about his family, she could inquire with a little more pressure than with Snacks, but not much more. It's true that she handled her boyfriend with a light grade of kid gloves, which she was now realizing probably brought him some Oedipal comfort, but she had no real fear of upsetting him with prying questions. She took much comfort in this truth and considered it as part of their strong relationship's foundation.

Thus she began again with: *What about like when you first got your apartment with Snacks? How was it living with him there?*

I don't know. The same?

Sensing resistance, she shifted gears with: *Where was he living before that?*

Before we got our place... Me, Snacks, Isaac and Stanley were the last ones at home with mom and dad. My dad joked that Snacks got a fire under his ass when he realized Stanley was going to be going to college, I was moving out, and he might be left there with just them two once Isaac moved on.

You were going to live with Bart at that time?

Yeah, and Snacks kept bugging me about letting him move in with us. I told him it was a two-bedroom and obviously the two were filled. It was super small, too, so when we got settled and he started staying over on the couch all the time, we barely had any space. I figured he would see for himself how there wasn't really room for him, but he just kept crashing there.

So then you just let him move in?

Pretty much. He was just always there and I figured we could use that huge break on the rent, especially when Isaac started asking to move-in. We were super broke at the time.

Angie waited for a beat before asking, *But they never paid rent, at least not regularly, right?*

No, they were pretty bad about it, replied Jack, completely missing the point.

Yeesh, she added to land the conversation. This was still pleasant news to her because she knew Snacks lacked ambition, but he did seem susceptible to some form of influence in the form of the stigma of being stuck as the only son still living with his parents. It seemed that shame was the route to take. But how do you shame someone who's forced his way into living in his younger brother's new home and was performing his role of tenant in an increasingly obstinate way. Wasn't that shameful enough? She hadn't even got to this part, but Snacks also hadn't even paid any rent yet. They agreed upon a fair $500/month to cover basic utilities and such, and Snacks looked her right in the eye when he accepted. Angie made the mistake of blaming herself for not asking him and keeping him honest, and every month, her self-blame only grew, making it more and more difficult to collect. Now they were over half a year into this arrangement to the point where it was extremely awkward because she didn't know if she should be asking for back pay, or just start fresh.

Why are you so interested in Snacks' childhood?, Jack laughed as he turned off the TV.

I don't know, I never hear about him in your stories. Him or Stanley.

Jack quickly informed: *Yeah, Snacks and Stanley always kept to themselves. I was probably the only one Stanley really talked to, to be honest.*

Why you?

Think because I was the closest in age. He was the baby and I had just been the baby, so I was like a mentor, I guess.

Angie did not need to clarify with Jack because she already knew very well that it was more than that. Jack and Stanley got along because they were both kind, selfless men. Perhaps the same could not be said for his oldest brother, but truth be told, men like Jack and Stanley were a rarity regardless. Although she had never met the youngest Norossi and truly had never heard any story of him whatsoever, she knew all she needed to know about him by the simple fact that he had a rapport with her beloved.

Instead of pressing him for more about his brother, she let Jack peacefully drift off. She reached over and shut off the lights to hasten the departure. However, she found it hard to shut down with all of this new information to process. Being the tactical mastermind that she was, she began workshopping new ways to approach Snacks. She was thinking much beyond moving the boxes now, but about establishing a dynamic that would resemble that of a parent, even though he was many years her senior. Essentially, she wanted the authority and the respect, but not at the cost of coming off as a hard ass. She, of course, didn't realize that she was dealing with the same challenge nearly all parents encounter--well, maybe not Mama Norossi. This was her house after all and she had the authority within its walls, but what a boorish manner of living to act like that. She had built her entire life around being a strong woman who never backed down from positions of influence, but also one who never ramrodded her way through her problems. She just needed a little more creativity is all. Yes, in the following days, she would come up with something that would re-establish the power dynamics in an effective manner that would please all parties. Until then, she would get a good night's sleep next to the man of her dreams.

Both Jack's parents and Angie's mother had made it clear that the amount of time that had passed since their move-in was unacceptable in that they had yet to be invited to a proper housewarming party. They did give them a certain amount of leeway due to their demanding careers and such, but there was a timeline for these things and to not have the family over for a get-together where they could have a tour and gift the new homeowners some basic necessities was just distasteful. Angie's sisters didn't help the matter by teaming with their mother at a brunch gathering

35

and expressing their desire to visit and party with the famous Norossis, who were regaled for their celebration acumen. However, on the bright side, it was this very ambush that pushed Angie into the next stage in her plan to get Snacks to clean up his lingering mess and slowly, but surely start to fall in line.

The next morning, she decided on a fool-proof tactic. She would print out a little memo for "everyone" in the house, so Snacks didn't feel singled out, and simply attach it to the fridge. All it said was that this Saturday would be a perfect day to give the house a little clean and spruce up before they had a small family gathering--a soft opening of sorts. No one would be forced to attend the cleaning, but there would be free beer and pizza involved for all those who dedicated their time and effort. If that was still not enticing enough, then so be it, just please have personal effects clear of public areas by Saturday night to allow the household to complete the purging without interference. She ended it by thanking the boys for their cooperation.

Snacks must not have eaten for the next five days, because not only did he not show up for the cleaning day, but his boxes were still in the living room bright and early Sunday morning. This is exactly what Angie had feared and honestly what she expected. It was becoming very clear that Snacks was very adept at getting out of duties, as in he has spent more than likely decades refining his ability to skirt anything and everything that even sounded like it would inconvenience him. Jack had told her that his brother had been indoctrinated from childhood with the concept that he was in full control of his world, but this blatant disrespect was undeniable truth that he truly believed he was above any rule whatsoever.

Angie did have to admit that most people overestimated the amount of control they had over their lives. People tend to believe that they can heavily influence aspects of their being such as relationships, economic status, level of happiness and fulfillment, and much more. And they believe they can do this any time they want. In fact, her generation received a lot of flack for being told from an early age that they were in control of their destiny. To her, it was quite obvious that humans have much less control than they think they have and the wisest philosophers, spiritual leaders, and learned of the race preached this incessantly. However, with a loaded arsenal of manipulative techniques, Snacks had made it through nearly fifty years of being able to influence his entire life within his desires, at least to an extent that he saw as satisfactory.

Angie was unaware, but Snacks had succeeded on several occasions in avoiding responsibility from authorities much more capable than her. Yes, his mother had introduced him to the concept, but it was his second grade teacher, Ms. Ruth, who gave him the chance to really cut his teeth. The school had a policy where the students had to place their homework assignments on her desk upon entering the classroom for the day. Ms. Ruth was clever in offering a gold star sticker to the first student to turn in his or her work, which not only kept a child consistent in completing their duties, but also in taking pride in exceptional punctuality. Gold Star stickers were displayed publicly and they were granted for a variety of accomplishments, but simply putting one's paper into the bin first was by far the easiest and one a student could earn every single day.

Long story short, Snacks was perpetually late to class, but this flaw was not necessarily his fault since it was his father's job (as bestowed by his mother) to drive him and he often overslept due to his late work hours. On top of this, he was not a particularly gifted student nor one who was keen on working hard, or even following basic directions. This made earning Stars very difficult and it did not take long for him to start to feel the shame of being at the bottom percentile of students not just in grades or general likeability, but also in something as meaningless, yet so very important, as Gold Stars.

Child Snacks needed a plan. He had already tried many times to wake up his father earlier and even threatened to walk his darn self to school early, but that was never going to fly under his protective mother. He figured that he needed to insert his influence in some way that happened after the school day started. There must be a way in which he could get his assignment in that bin first. (Finishing the assignment was no issue at all, of course, because even if he didn't feel like doing that work, his mother or one of his younger brothers would just finish it for him.)

One day, he figured it out. Ms. Ruth always checked the bin after the Pledge of Allegiance and the roll call. He needed to strike within that time window. It was so simple: hold onto the paper until she was distracted and then slip it under the others. There were just some details to iron out, but it would surely be nothing the brilliant eight-year-old couldn't handle.

The plan was simple. First, Snacks complained to Ms. Ruth that he was having trouble seeing the board, so that he would be able to move to the seat in front right by her desk. She was thrilled since Snacks was an underperforming student and his desire to facilitate his education was great news indeed. Once relocated, Snacks then began studying Ms. Ruth's morning routine. What he found was that after the Pledge of Allegiance, she dug in her bag for the binder with the attendance sheet in it. This took about forty seconds give or take because of its weight and the amount of documents she held in there. This was perfect because the kid only needed ten seconds to drop the paper in the assignment bin. Now, he knew how to execute the swap, but how would he sell it when he always walked into the classroom after they had started the Pledge? Well, this required some more creativity, but he solved it as easily as leaving his jacket on the back of his chair and an empty backpack on the floor at the end of the day. He had to be the last to leave the classroom to pull this off, but if he did, he could just stroll in when he pleased and if he was asked about his tardiness, he would lie that he was present before the bell, and he had just exited quickly to use the restroom.

Finally, there was the last issue of suck ups who might see him switch the paper and tell on him. There were Gold Stars at stake after all, so the top students would be quick to interrupt his scheme that would cheat them out of their reward. Luckily, Snacks was a bully by nature, so the weaker, smarter kids already knew to keep their mouths shut. The lower tier students didn't care about gold stars, so that just left the upper-mid kids, which he could intimidate or bribe with the appropriate Hostess pastry as needed.

The following Monday, Snacks chatted up Ms. Ruth when the final bell rang and kept her attention enough to leave his jacket and backpack. The next day, he ironically strolled into class--theatrically "drying" his hands with his bathroom paper towel prop--right when they were at the "Justice for All" part of the Pledge, and when the children sat down and Ms. Ruth leaned over to grab the attendance book, Snacks dropped his assignment underneath the pile. When she finally got around to checking the stack, she flipped it over and paused at seeing his homework there first. After a beat, she announced that Snacks earned the Gold Star and went about the lesson plan as normal. He got away with that for the rest of the year and ended up only four Gold Stars short of being the top of the class.

Multiply this by every teacher/boss/coach, and you can start to imagine just what Angie was up against. This was a master of his craft who had spent enough years studying that he could now give symposiums on how to influence one's fellow man. In reality, she should have just been glad she was not on his bad side because who knows what he would do if he decided to use this skill set against her, or for any evil in general. A stack of boxes in the front room was getting off easy when one looked at it from that perspective.

It was a real shame that Angie was not able to know about Snacks' path to mastery because if she had, she would have known not to make the major mistake that she did. After coming to the conclusion that she was making too big a deal about a stack of cardboard, she decided to just take the two minutes to drag them into his room. If he was upset by the intrusion, too bad. She was doing him a favor and more importantly, it was her living room. So she went ahead and cleaned out the space, placing his boxes in his room and finally finishing that deep clean.

Snacks never mentioned the moving of his boxes and Angie never saw them again. It had appeared on the surface that the problem was over and that the household was ready to move on and live peacefully, as expected. One factor in her decision to just clean the mess herself was that, outside of that detail, Snacks was a fine tenant. There were really no complaints from either her or Jack outside of some harmless messiness. So, why shouldn't she just take action and reclaim her peace?

It is only natural that problems arise in life, and that they arrive in different degrees of intensity. However, they often share a similar pattern in that our biggest problems grow out of belittling our smaller ones. Ignore that CHECK ENGINE light and it could cost you significantly more time and money than it would have if you had just taken it into the shop right away. There are millions of examples where we see this, and they do not get easier when it comes to relationships, especially ones as delicate as familial bonds. It's the irony of the "easy way". It actually doesn't exist. Shortcuts do not lead to the same path that hard work does. Half-assed work creates a circle that will keep you repeating the same problems over and over again until you either learn or run out of time completely. Angie didn't know it then, but the absolute worst thing she could have done was move those boxes herself. Snacks may be a master of elusiveness, but now she personally established a dangerous precedent. The fact was: she took the easy way--the quick fix. Instead of confronting this man, preferably with the help of his brother, she chose to enable him further. Truth be told, Snacks was in desperate need of a reality check and Angie could have given him that priceless gift right then and there. The stars were pretty much aligned for her to do so. However, even perfect little Angela Saccomanno can make mistakes, and some are bigger than others. The cruel twist of fate would be that in Angie avoiding her chance to teach Snacks a highly valuable lesson, she would in turn be taught a lesson of high worth herself.

THE DOGS

Rarely is it disputed that time is unfair, but it's especially grievous in how quickly it passes. It neither concerns itself with how much one enjoys the current state of being or with how much one will suffer through the upcoming state. The clock simply keeps on ticking and everything around us changes second-by-second.

Perhaps we spend too much of our limited time with activities designed to drain it. We work forty or more hours a week at our primary income generators, take vacations often prescribed in one week intervals (often twice per year), raise children that eat up eighteen (or more) years, and sign mortgages that often lock us into payments for thirty or more laps around the sun. That last one is a third of some lifetimes. Then again… what else would we do with that time? Snacks might in reality be a pioneering genius when it comes to the deeper fundamental understanding of time and space. He had discovered that the best use of one's finite time on Earth is to simply waste it all.

Angie had originally wanted to ask Jack for his brother Stanley's address, but she didn't want any incriminating follow-up questions and honestly, she wasn't even sure if she would go through with it.

The Saccomanno girls had a tradition of writing letters to each other. This started the first time Bee went off to Fort Lauderdale to spend the summer with her best friend at the time and her family. The girls were so close that they cried and cried for weeks before her departure, tortured by the thought of not having their Big Sis with them to chase down ice cream trucks and give them the once-over to make sure they were sufficiently screened from the sun. Most of all, they squirmed at the concept of not staying up all night and listening to her famous ghost stories. With no bedtimes in the summer, Charlie and Angie had believed they once again had a limitless supply of scares just waiting to keep them up late into the night. Now, all their plans were null and void… that is, until Bee hatched one of her many brilliant ideas. She would swear to write (at least) one scary story for her sisters every week she was gone.

This promise played into Bee's natural writing tendencies and before they knew it, the California girls could expect two, three, sometimes up to five letters nearly every day, and they were sending out just as many back to Broward County. The habit continued any time one of the three was away and naturally, continues today as the three girls are now women with their own lives.

This particular correspondence also allowed for a special kind of conversation where one party could say their entire piece without interruption or the often-unbalanced ebb and flow of a normal conversation. This was very therapeutic and allowed for a nice change of pace from the more popular texting or even auditory communication. Add in the fact that one had the barrier of time and distance, along with no need to see the writer's face, and you had the perfect and unrivaled balance to divulge.

This is exactly why Angie thought it would be fun and appropriate to reach out to the stranger, Stanley Norossi, via a letter.

She had wanted to speak with the distant brother ever since she heard about his reclusiveness, but when Jackson mentioned that he was the only brother who had a rapport with him, she knew she had her in. Plus she had to invite him to the home at some point anyway. So, she went ahead and used girlfriend (or co-owner) privilege and dug up his Miami address and put pen to paper.

Dear Stanley,

I imagine that you're surprised to see my name in your mailbox. Nice to meet you! (I hope you've heard of me.) I've heard so much about you! I'm writing you because I just wanted to touch base a little. Hope this finds you at a good time. I feel like I'm spending more and more time with all of your brothers and I feel a little sad that we've never spoken. I know you're a busy man with lots of cool things going on and I thought I'd be the first to say hi.

Hope you appreciate the letter too, emails are so sterile and meh, right?

Well, I don't want to bother you too much and honestly, please don't feel like you're being compelled to write back, even though I would love to be pen pals! (No pressure whatsoever.)

-- Angie

P.S. We'll be having a sort of housewarming at some point soon and we'd love to see you there! More info to come!

...

As much as it surprised all three inhabitants, the one year anniversary of their residency was coming up very quickly. They had seen their seasonal cycle once through and it had already felt as if they had been here their whole lives. For the most part, stasis had been achieved and there were no real disputes to mention. This understanding had come about organically. Angela knew how to pick her battles with Snacks, knowing that Jack was not going to lay down the law at any point, and Snacks knew how to avoid getting Angela to the red line. Well, he would get her right up against that line, but never over it. It was in this Mexican stand-off manner that the household had established a cease-fire and kept its own definition of peace.

There was one lingering issue that Angie was determined to resolve this very month. As ludicrous as it might have sounded, Snacks still had not paid a dime in rent thus far. Once again, they had verbally agreed on a set amount of $500 to cover housing and utilities, and to be honest a ton of meals too, since Angie always set a plate for Snacks at dinner. This meant that Jack's brother had not only been living for free, but he had been eating a lot of the food they paid for, and using the water/gas/pool/electricity/wifi/etc completely gratis. Angela was afraid that this was bordering on theft since Snacks most definitely should be the one to hand her (or Jack) that check on the first of every month simply out of respect and decency. It was quite unfair for him to force Angela's hand in the sure-to-be awkward pressing for the cash.

Angie talked it over with Jack and he agreed that it was obviously not good for Snacks to live freely in their home, even if he did take the trash out every once in a while. He suggested they just ask Snacks to do more chores around the house to earn his keep, but Angie immediately shot this down. The same error occurs when parents try to tie their children's allowance to their chores. Often times, the chores are done piss poorly, or skipped altogether when the child has enough funds to afford to abdicate. Snacks would probably do a poor job at anything he attempted since he didn't have many skills, and he would of course not stick to a maintenance schedule because he doesn't stick to any schedule. That arrangement would force Angie to have to hound him constantly to do every single maintenance request and it would become an exercise in the absurd of her trying to force Snacks to do what he already agreed upon, so she told Jack to just forget that option. Instead, they decided that they would simply ask Snacks to deliver his first $500 check in three weeks' time when the calendar changed, and he would of course not be required to pay any past months' dues. He might consider that a gift for… whatever he wants it to be.

The next morning everyone had the day off. Angie woke up, made her coffee, and read her book amidst the peace and quiet. Her boyfriend had already confirmed that they would speak to Snacks about the rent today, and if he was unable to be reached, Jack himself would text him about it and they would go from there. Even though it had been a bit of a rough ride with Snacks until this point, Angela was feeling good about this because she finally had Jack on her side. It wasn't so much that he wasn't on her side the times before, but he hadn't given her the support she desired. Now, she would not admit this, but that irked her more than she let on.

Of course, by this point she was having major regrets about allowing Snacks to move in, but it was more problematic with how she had to deal with him by herself. This was after all his brother, not hers. Jack had the benefit of being used to his brother's quirks and his arsenal of tricks, but that was no excuse to leave his girlfriend to fend for herself. They always say that living with someone will bring you very close, and many times this is closer than one would like. She was now starting to see some qualities in her lover that were not perfect, but she was obviously wise enough to realize that no one was perfect and these deficiencies were certainly preferable to others. This was just a passing thought that caught her when she had her guard down, and she was sure it would ameliorate itself in time.

It was in this alone time actually that Angie was best able to put her worries at ease. There had been many times in her childhood home, dorms, and apartments where she was never able to secure true alone time. Now with her own home, she could essentially have alone time whenever she pleased and it was arguably the best thing about living there. She was actually in the middle of a sip of her French Roast, as she expressed her gratitude for that particular blessing. She, no doubt, had much for which to be thankful and she did her best to take an active role in her gratitude for every last stroke of good fortune. That was what it was after all: fortune. One wrong decision or random act could have sent her down a completely different path. It could have also sent Jack down a different path that didn't intersect hers. She could go crazy thinking about this, but what exactly did make Jack so different from his brother? Why was he so responsible and organized when his brother was so... lost?

Right as she found herself going down this long, tumultuous line of thinking, she heard a scurrying down the hallway. These weren't the subtle slide of Jack's socks, or the slap of Snacks' bare feet, but instead almost like really low-heeled women's shoes. Angie was a mere moment

47

from flipping out with the thought that Snacks had brought a girl to her home. She never was clear about the no girls policy, but this surely should have been assumed. Especially because she figured she had enough evidence to gain that the only kind of women that would be persuaded to share a bed with Snacks would have to be either terribly desperate… or be paid by the hour. It was not her place to judge either party, but still.

Honestly, she didn't know what she would say or do if in fact a prostitute emerged in her living room. She didn't want to know what she''d do. Out of instinct, she stood up and unbeknownst to herself, took a fighting stance. She began even walking toward the hall to meet the origin head on, but she was surprised to see nothing in her eye line. The sound continued clacking as its creator made its way toward Angie, who dropped to a knee to greet her.

In her hands was a puppy dog. The beast was some sort of doberman mix with slick black fur and a lean build. She had been drawn to Angie and was bombarding her with kisses and cuddles despite this being their first meeting. The dog was a striking one, and she didn't have a tag so she must have been a stray. Whatever the reason, it was a pleasant surprise to Angie's gorgeous morning and she welcomed it with little to no apprehension. She spent the rest of her morning sitting with the new pup at her feet, waiting for the ensuing explanation.

When both boys had risen, she finally got the story. Snacks claims that he heard noises in the back by the garage and he got up to check it out. Long story short, there was a lone pup digging in the trash. She looked frightened, but did not run away. Snacks said that she was probably starving and had almost no energy to escape the potential threat. He brought her in the backyard, fried up a few eggs, poured some water in a bowl, and watched as the poor beast replenished her diminishing substrate levels. After finishing her meal, the dog followed Snacks around, but would not go back outside to the alley. It was very cold so this was understandable and Snacks could not bring himself to leave the poor animal to bear the elements, so he put a blanket on the day

48

room couch, and let her fall asleep. She quickly curled up and drifted off into a deep slumber.

Jack absolutely loves dogs and had even brought up the idea of having a full pack of them when they were considering this house. At present, he was drowning this pup in pets and baby talk, which Angie found unfathomably adorable. There was definitely a discussion to be had, but it was clear that the dog was staying. The only real discussion of worth was what to call her. She was a striking specimen with the most adorable deep brown eyes and a perpetual smile, so this was quite the task. What name could encapsulate such a sweet, beautiful miracle dog? Jack suggested that since Snacks was the true savior, he should be given the honor to name her. Angie agreed, reserving the right to veto, of course. He kneeled in front of the dog, who ran to him immediately, gave her a nice ear tuffle, looked deep into her eyes and said one word. It was as simple as that for a man who made absolutely every single life decision off pure intuition. Thus, in a moment that quick, they had added a new tenant to the home. From now on, every day when Angie, Jack, or Snacks arrived home, they would be greeted by the marvelous and fate-favored pooch that would answer to the name *Bella*.

It was only natural that Bella would grow closest to Snacks. Not only was he her savior, but since both Jack and Angie worked high level jobs, it was Snacks who was home the most often. He fed her everyday, took her for walks, and even cleaned up her "discharges". Snacks spent the time to train her how to sit, fetch, and stop barking when required. Honestly, Jack even admitted that he had never seen his brother become so attentive with anyone. There was something about Bella that they all loved, but Snacks had found a real buddy in that dog and it was the perfect fit for all involved.

One day in particular, Angie had just come home from work when she saw Snacks playing with Bella outside. She always had a flair for the dramatic, but with the sun just starting to set and their beautiful pup jumping into the air to catch her toy, then running back so damn majestically to a flurry of pets, it was hard to forget that you weren't watching a Hallmark movie. She became more introspective at this sight and thought to herself how her and Jack's hard work and focus had given this poor animal a home where she could thrive. The thing was... as amazing as this gift of a home was for Bella, it was equally, if not more, depressing for Snacks.

In many ways, Snacks was like their pet. First of all, he paid exactly as much rent as Bella did. They fed him regularly, had to clean up after him at times, and he used a lot of their stuff without replacing it. Sure, he was a little more self-sufficient than a dog, but not by much. Seeing him with Bella like this made it all the more apparent. She "rescued" Snacks, but this wasn't a good thing when one did it for a grown man. By giving him a home and letting him squeak by all the time, she was continuing to cripple him.

Although he may have convinced himself in some way that he was the master of his fate because he could wiggle out of so many different kinds of situations, all one had to do was look at the net score to see that he was so far behind it was pitiful. He was almost fifty years old with no wife, no kids, no home of his own, a very low-paying job, and not much else. His manipulation had damaged himself more than anyone else, and Angie began to wonder that if she was just realizing this, had he?

She walked over to the two, careful not to infringe too abruptly.

Hey guys, she said, quickly turning her tone back to its default positive.

Hey Angie, Snacks replied, then commanded Bella, *Say hi to your mom*. Bella sprinted over into Angie's arms and was absorbed by her "mother" who showered her in praise. After reveling in the love, the hound made its way back to Snacks for further instruction.

What a gorgeous day, huh? Glad you guys are enjoying it, she said.

Oh yeah, we went for a quick run up the street earlier. There's a nice hill if you go up Hunsucker past 18th. Kind of brutal, but this one's a grinder.

For a man in such dismal circumstances, he spoke with such confidence. It baffled Angie to an extent she was sure surpassed whatever effect, if any, it had on the man himself. Did any of this bother him? Living in his baby brother's house? Seeing all of his siblings, cousins, and even their children pass him in maturation? Having to see all of his co-workers stay the same age, while every day he came into work older? Was it really possible that this adult man was happy--even content--with this life? At least enough to just stop trying and say "well, this is good enough"?

She was neck deep in her overthinking by this point and began to lay the groundwork for her theory of how Snacks might be using Bella to express his desire or even his need to father something. Obviously, Angie and Jack were not even married, but the process had been initiated and surely they would have a kid within the next five to seven years, which would at the latest make Jack a father by his late thirties. Fortunately for men, age wasn't as restrictive as it was for women, but Snacks needed to check like four MAJOR boxes before he could even think about supporting a child, and he seemed to be in no rush to check any of them.

She just took right to you, huh?

Never one to boast about his tact, Snacks replied with: *Yeah. I'm sure feeding her, walking her, and playing with her is a big part, too.*

This didn't necessarily offend Angie, but it did seem to be a bit barbed. Anyway, It was enough to remind her that he needed to pay rent next month. However, she was tactful enough to not outright say this, but instead dive into the deeper issues, albeit very carefully.

So how's your job going? she asked as she took a seat on the nearby lounge chair.

Same bullshit, you know. That manager is ten years younger than me telling me how to make a schedule. He's only been manager for like six months, but he wants to show that he could take command or whatever. So I just play along. Makes my life easier. It is what it is.

A thing to know about Snacks was that although he was not much of a talker, and he had a hermit tendency, you could always get him to talk if you gave him an opportunity to complain. As is the case with most unhappy people, they jump at the chance to explain to you EXACTLY, and in rich detail, as to why the entire world has conspired against them for the sole reason to keep them down.

Angie added, *Yeah, he's probably a weak guy trying too hard to establish his authority. I told you to take that position when they wanted to give it to you.*

Sheeeeiiit. I don't want that job. Kid barely makes more than me and has to pull fifty-sixty hour weeks all the time. They send him to meetings all over the IE just to sit there and listen to suits tell him how to do his job. Hell no.

Guess you're right, Angie relented, pausing for a beat, then getting to another point. *What do you got going on tonight? A hot date?*

Shit, if you see Carmella, you haven't seen me, alright? he laughed.

Aw. I liked her. Does that mean you guys are totally done? Wait, don't tell me you found someone else.

No, I'm worn out, man. Can't keep up with these girls. Too much drama, you know?

Angie hesitated but even she couldn't restrain herself to ask: *Well, how are you gonna get married and have your family if you don't deal with the drama?*

You mean, when am I gonna meet a girl and move out?

Oh my god, that's not what I mean, she quickly lied. *I'm just saying when I see you with Bella and all the other little Norossi nephews, figured you'd be looking forward to having some of your own.*

Who knows?

As he started to clam up, she thought it might be time to lay off... but she kept going instead. It might have been that she found this a proper way to get back at him by making him uncomfortable with a line of questioning that surfaces issues that he probably spends a good deal of time repressing. Or maybe she was just that curious. Either way, she continued with: *What do you want in life?*

What kind of question is that?

I just mean like for example: I want kids. I want a family. I also want more in my career. I want to eventually retire and take my grandkids to Disneyland every other weekend, and spend weeks in Greece, Japan, Brazil, whatever. I'm just curious what it is you want if it's not kids or companionship, or whatever most people say they want.

Snacks bounced Bella's ball in front of him for a while, keeping his head down. Then quickly muttered: *Psssh. I don't think about stuff like that. I'm gonna grill some chicken later, did you want some?*

The quickturn in conversation signaled for Angie to stop, and this time she did. She stared at her future brother-in-law just bouncing that ball over and over like a child. His old t-shirt with its faded Big Dogs logo and his basketball shorts fluttering gently in the wind. Perhaps for the first time, she saw that he was trapped. Not just in life, but in his current mental state. They cleverly call it arrested development, which conveys the concept that much like when being held in a jail cell, there is no immediate escape, and there might not be any escape at all.

Indeed, he ran from those thoughts because if they ever reached him, he would be tortured by the truth that he could never achieve any of his goals--at least that's what he convinced himself, which was a cop out of the most intricate nature. She was certain he had plenty of those ready to fire anytime he needed them.

No, I'm fine. Thank you, she responded as she stood up and made her way inside.

Angie was a problem-solver by nature. She had never been afraid to dive in and put her skills to use in helping some person or system correct its path and work to its best ability. She would be a fantastic mother because of this tendency, and she knew it well. One should be careful though, because she would quite literally murder Snacks before assuming the role of his mother. In fact, his problems were likely rooted in the fact that he was over-mothered in the first place. However, she did have in front of her an opportunity to mentor this man. What else was she supposed to do? He was a tax on the household and the only thing that made it somewhat less annoying was to think that this was part of the "greater plan" in that Snacks needed Angie to force him to grow up, and in turn give him the tools and mindset to achieve what he really wanted, and what he was afraid to admit that he wanted.

It all made sense really, because the only way to help Snacks was to be tough with him. This was a challenge in itself because she didn't have the experience in making people do things that he had in avoiding doing things, but she was always up for the biggest of trials.

Step one in this process was the same step that obviously needed to be taken and should have been taken first: collecting rent. Angie was convinced, but she was missing the big picture in this instance. Even if she did get Snacks to pay rent on time every month, what would happen in a year's time, two years? Would she really have kids in this house with Snacks just hanging out? She repressed this firmly, but there would come a time when they would need to ask Snacks to leave. She really should have never let him move in, but the next best action would be to kick him out right now because every moment she waited, he grew older and less able to adapt to the change. With every moment she delayed, to make it easier on herself, she made it harder on him, and this would then make it harder on Jack to back her up. The cycle would eventually make its way back to her and the ouroboros of her own creation would swallow her whole. On top of that, this "easy way out" would put tiny cracks in their relationship because there was no way Jack would understand the act of mercy that would be kicking out his kin. After all, he didn't even think there was a problem.

There were a lot of very precise moves that needed to be taken, and it really was too bad that she couldn't see the long-term effects of each one. If she did have that power, she could have avoided so many of her biggest mistakes that followed.

The following morning, Angie saw a pile of mail on the table and was elated to find new handwriting on one of the envelopes. Despite the plain packaging and sterile pre-printed return address, she tossed the other mail to the side and even delayed the opening of the sparkly purple correspondence from Bee to erratically rip open the surprise:

Dear Angela:

Nice to meet you, as well. I'm flattered that you took time to write to me and I want to say right away that I am absolutely interested in being your pen pal.

I would also love to see your home. Please let me know as soon as you have a scheduled date for a housewarming party. As you may have heard, I get terribly busy in Miami and I very rarely get to come out west, but please send me all details and I'll do my best to work it in.

Now... I have to ask how it is dealing with TWO Norossi boys. I'm sure by now I don't have to elaborate on why I'm asking. You also have Raphael with you, and he's probably the most "Norossi" of us all. No need to spare my feelings. Seriously, I'm very curious.

Anyway, thanks again for writing to me. It was a nice surprise and it gave me an excuse to get away from my work. Sometimes, I get glued to my screen and forget that there's a whole world out there. Even in my line of work, it's easy to get lost in the doledrum.

I'll be anxiously awaiting your next letter.

-- Stanley

P.S. Just to save you some trouble. Be aware that Snacks' recurring urinary tract infections are not as severe as he says they are, and they're brought on by his own negligence. I learned early on that he leans on that excuse more than it actually afflicts him. Jack still thinks I'm heartless for saying this, but I think you should be aware, just in case.

...

Jack was a homebody by nature and he frankly didn't like to travel at all. This is one reason why Las Vegas and San Francisco were such hot spots for the couple. It was actually one of Angie's pet peeves that Jack was terrified of flying. She tried with earnest to forget the fact that the man who she so desperately wanted to marry and spend her life beside was one that needed several tranquilizers and a few shots of 80 proof just to board a commercial airliner.

Jackson's aerophobia was the primary, although not the lone, reason as to why he was so tense before his upcoming business trip. The firm he served was sending their top account men to Minnesota for a conference on social media strategy, and even though Jack only ever worked with traditional print marketing, he was the go-to guy in his department, so he had to attend.

Another issue that made him reluctant to attend was the fact that Minnesota was cold as all hell, and Jack detested the cold. Most of the time, these things were held in nicer places just far enough from LA to sound exotic like San Diego or Santa Barbara. They were usually two-day events that the firm was happy to pay accommodation for, but Jack liked his bed and even if it meant a few less hours in it, he would avoid the hotels at all cost. Now he would be forced to spend a few days in a hotel that he had to fly to, in a freezing cold tundra, and with a bunch of people he did not really care for. On top of all this, he would have to leave Angela home alone for the first time since they've lived together.

It was times like these that Jack was especially thankful that he had Snacks at home. Not only was Jack helpless when it came to basic maintenance, but he didn't even know how to contact someone to do that kind of thing. Fortunately for him, he had an older brother like Snacks who knew the in's and out's of DIY and basic housecraft, and thus he never needed to worry himself.

And now, Jack could take his business trip without a worry that anything would happen to Angie, all thanks to his big brother.

Angela didn't care whether Snacks was there or not, but she did want to make sure that he didn't think he could blast his music, leave his trash out, have the boys over, and leave this house a wasteland just because the man of the house was out. She didn't anticipate he would go this far since she would still be home (thank god), but she would rather let him know upfront so he couldn't defend himself with ignorance. Jack assured her that he would go over everything with his brother before he left, but she took little comfort in this reassurance, despite accepting it without protest. She was starting to feel that Jack was forgetting this weekend would be hard for her, too. She had only grown more attached and even more in love with him since their cohabitation and now they would be apart for the first time since it started. For one, there was an emotional strain involved just in having to say goodbye, then there was the more tangible one in having to fall asleep alone and not see him first thing upon opening her eyes. There was also the added obstacle in how she didn't want to tell Jack this because she didn't want to transfer this trouble to him when he already had much to worry about himself. So, she internalized it, accepted his reassurances, and prepared for the lonely set of days.

The first day had gone surprisingly fast. This was probably because Angie had made a list about three pages long of errands to occupy her. She made her way across town getting her nails done, a fresh batch of groceries, a few volunteer hours in, and even made time to visit her favorite park across town to just sit and read a bit--something she had not done in years. The list had occupied such a huge chunk of her time that she arrived home well past sunset. As she exited the car and opened the door into her home, she took an excessive amount of care into the act. She was not necessarily afraid of what lied beyond the doorway, but she did not want to see anything she could not unsee. With Snacks around, there was no telling what would be going on.

Fortunately, there was nothing. Literally. The house was quiet and dark. Snacks must not have been home since he had the annoying habit of turning all the house lights on at like 16:00, when the sun was clearly still up. Angie proceeded to make a quick dinner, watch the end of the Angels' game, and then decided she might as well pass the time by heading to bed and grabbing a few extra hours of sleep.

This plan worked flawlessly… for about three hours.

It was at about 02:00 when she heard a concert of voices emanating from some place far too close for Angie's comfort. At first very apprehensive, she calmed a very small amount when she recognized Snacks' voice as among them. He was in the backyard, and there were two-maybe-three voices among them. This was her worst fear, well not her WORST fear, but a fear nonetheless.

She got out of bed and carefully crept to the sliding door, where she was strategizing on how exactly to peek past the curtain and see who her tenant had brought to her home without permission. For now she could hear that they were meeting Bella. Snacks' voice became velvety and amplified as he bragged about how he saved her and how Jack had let him name her. One voice was complimenting him on how well trained she was. The other was saying something about how these kinds of dogs were the best guard dogs.

That's when she heard a can open. Angie began to entertain a panic, thinking they were just starting their party. How many more were coming over? Were there going to be drugs in her house? She really had no idea and that was not a position she liked occupying. To add to this, she was still about 13% asleep which was making all of this feel like it was happening much faster than it actually was. She quickly made the decision that this was her house (Damn it!), and she does not need to be coy about seeing who's coming over. She has the right, and duty, to go out there and find out just what the hell is going on. It was better to do this right now anyway, before the potential drug dealers arrived. So, without stopping to overthink, she slid the door open and headed outside.

Right away, she saw Jack's brother Paul and their family friend, Caleb. The tension only elevated as they waited for her to speak. When that didn't happen, they both offered their hello's, then immediately apologized for waking her. She waved off the disturbance and relayed how good it was to see them. Angie welcomed them inside, but they declined, not wanting to impose. Snacks told the guys that it was late and they should probably head out, but she stopped him right there and said that they of course could stay and hang out if they wanted. It was the weekend and she was up anyway just playing on her phone. Coyly, she added that she had heard a beer open and that they might as well finish it inside. Caleb then produced his tall can energy drink, which brought a forced smile to her face. After joking about how she can't believe these boys weren't drinking, she told them she should stop bugging and head back to her room, but warned them not to be extra quiet on her account.

It was obvious that she had spoiled the mood beyond repair and the two repeated their intent to leave. Angie insisted they come back next weekend to have some beers as Snacks led them out the back gate where their car was parked. She couldn't be sure but he seemed to be rushing them and of course, she had no idea what he was telling them once they were out of ear shot.

However, instead of letting her own half-conscious imagination ruin the evening even further than her half-conscious actions already had, she headed back inside, tucked herself under her warm sheets, and was blessed to fall asleep before the thoughts of how she was becoming an overreacting tyrant just like her mother could creep into her head.

•••

It was once more Angie's favorite time of the week, complete with hot coffee in her hands and the official Los Angeles Kings' podcast playing. Bella was running up and back the sun-soaked yard, as she often did on the weekends, when people were more inclined to walk along the alley behind her home.

It was Sunday and the only sports on TV were baseball (unrelated to the Angels) and lacrosse. Even though Angie had no allegiance, she figured that meant she could watch this fringe sport for pure entertainment, as opposed to when her teams played and she was biting her nails down to the bone the entire time. The first game was going to start soon and she was about ready to veg out for a few hours, that is once she finished this letter.

Naturally, she was thrilled to receive any reply whatsoever from her estranged future brother-in-law, but she had taken extra joy in how he specifically cited Snacks in the text. She could tell that he desperately wanted to divulge some more info on the man-child (UTI issues?) and she was ready to absorb it all. Of course, she couldn't just ask him for dirt or dig right in. She was still an outsider, after all. However, the opportunity had presented itself to get some more insight into the mind of Snacks, and of course, a little factoid here or there on her boyfriend would certainly not be turned away, either.

Dear Stanley,

First things first. The BBQ is on! The Sunday before Memorial Day, we'll be hosting your family and mine, so please please please do whatever you can to join. We would LOVE to have you (and a guest [or two], of course). Let me know if there's anything special you need.

You're right, your brothers are a handful, haha, but I'm sure I don't have to tell you that Jackson is amazing. He's doing so well at his job right now, (He

60

probably won't brag to you, so I will.) and he's really happy about it. It seems like it took forever, but his supervisors are finally treating him like the talent he is. He's travelling a bit more now and getting first looks at all their big accounts. It's very exciting to see where he's headed. I can only imagine what he'll do now that his team's full-on behind him.

In even better news, we finally have the house in some order and it's actually very nice. (Hence the BBQ plans.) I knew we'd love it here, but now that it's been a little while, it's like better than I could have ever thought. It feels like a "home", like family, like something you can't buy. You have to create it. Maybe I'm being too quick on the trigger in saying that, but I feel it, so it's at least that real. Again, PLEASE come to the BBQ. It's going to be epic.

Since you brought it up… "Snacks" is… well, himself. I know you know what that means. He's really great to have around. Honestly. But sometimes he's just like... "in the way". Like, he left his moving boxes around here for like a full year. I finally had to put them in his room for him! And between us… he's never paid any rent. I know it's my fault in a big way because I keep brushing it off, but still. Sometimes I can't believe him and Jack are brothers, but maybe you feel like that too? He does some things… like he just brought a dog home, like it's his house. I don't get how that thought comes to his head when he's never made one true financial contribution. Maybe he really does think bringing home a pizza once a month counts? Anyway, I don't want to rant. Jack tells me about how he was your mom's favorite and all that, and maybe he just got used to it. Whatever, I'm hoping things get better and maybe he

starts getting ready to move out some point soon. All I
can do is--

As she was wrapping up that thought, she heard the garage door
open. This was not surprising at all (outside of the fact that she was
"speaking/writing of the devil"), because Snacks was probably coming
back with breakfast, ONLY his of course. She tucked away the tab with
the in-progress letter and instinctively started gathering her things to take
into her room. However, as she was about to make her escape, something
unexpected sprinted out of the garage.

The pure white critter stopped in her tracks when she saw Angie.
Unlike Bella, she did not approach. In fact, she scurried over to the
corner to be as far away as possible from her while a second, much
bigger beast trotted past his buddy, right into Angie's arms. Once again,
she was distracted by the sheer novelty of the dogs to think, especially
when Bella trotted over to begin sniffing the new arrival and the two
shared the most adorable first meeting she had ever witnessed. Snacks
emerged from the door with a bag filled with dog toys and firstly
addressed the shy albino.

Nora, don't be rude. Go say hi to mama, he told the dog as he
made his way to the outside table to begin opening the new toys.

Where did these come from? Angie said as she drowned the
brown one in ear tussles. *I know her name's Nora. What's your name?*

*That one's Mark. Nora is his wife. It's a long story, but I figured
you wouldn't want more than two. There's a whole litter of puppies back
at Tim's.*

So… these are ours now?

*Well, you don't HAVE to keep them. I offered since we had the
room. I'll help you find someone to take them in if that's what you want.*

Angie stood up, trying to get her bearings with everything that
was happening way too fast. *Okay, what happened? Where are these
guys from?*

Tim is getting evicted. Well, don't tell anyone I told you, but his wife's kicking him out. He's got these two dogs and they had puppies a while back, so he still has a bunch of those he's trying to unload. As he's... transitioning, he's at a motel and he can't care for his dogs. Naturally, his wife wants nothing to do with anything involving Tim, so I told him we'd watch the two calmer ones for him.

So he's going to want them back?

I don't know. I doubt it, man. Tim's screwed. Snacks tossed a ball out for Mark, who sprinted over to grab it and bring it back. *His wife's gonna take everything. She thinks he has another girlfriend. Anyway, she's gonna be extra vicious. So, we can have them if we want.*

Does Jack know?

I was gonna surprise him. If that's okay with you. I was just thinking about it too. How it's kind of cruel to keep Bella here by herself. Dogs are pack animals. They don't like being alone. They seriously can get depressed. You see how she clings to you when you get home, right?

Yeah, but did we need two more? And you could've sent me a text or something.

I know. I know. That's why I told Tim we would watch them for a little bit. Like, he might want them back. Who knows?

Angie did not know what to say. This was a major breach across the line and it was completely unacceptable, but she knew that when Jack got home, he would go all googly-eyed and insist they keep them. Everything Snacks had said made logical sense, too. She couldn't catch him in his usual shaky line of thinking. This time he had been very careful in getting his story straight and he had her cornered. Even she was already falling in love with the two!

She looked over at Snacks, who carefully approached a very guarded Nora. He crouched, offered a treat, and spoke to the dog very gently, until she finally came over and sniffed his hand, and eventually allowed him to pet her. Snacks was good. He knew how to get what he wanted, and people (dogs, too) fell into line with his agenda very often because he framed it so that it looked like it was your agenda. As she realized she had no grounds to tell him to take the dogs back, she thought about how she didn't even want him to take them back. Bella needed a playmate. Jack would love them. The two shouldn't be separated. She would have done the same.

Snacks, she called to him. *Next time. Can you just let me know before you bring two big dogs home with you? It's fine, just... you should let me or Jack know before you volunteer our house.*

Definitely. Sorry about that. Like I said, I knew I could just bring them back to Tim if I had to. I'll call you next time. What happened was I was actually at the hospital--

Oh my god. What happened?

You know how I get those urinary infections? Did Jack tell you?

Angie must have reacted because Snacks changed his expression. This is what Stanley was alluding to in his previous letter. Snacks must have been feeling that he had crossed a line because he hadn't used this so-called excuse with her yet. She would pretend to know now, but later find out that he had a birth defect that somehow must have manifested in an infection-prone urethra and from what she understood, it was mostly an inconvenience, but it had put him out of work for spells. She thought it funny that Stanley knew his brother so well, he had been able to get just ahead of his games to warn her. Now, she would have to judge the bluff herself.

Yeah, she said, *was it bad?*

Ah, it's just a little one this time, he said as he pivoted out of the issue. *I'm fine. Don't worry. Anyway, I got their food and everything, too. I'll make sure they get walked and all that. I got it all covered.*

Angie smiled, half-heartedly. Yet again, she just wanted this interaction with her tenant to end, even if it meant granting him all of his terms. *Thanks*, she said as she started to head back into the house. *Oh,* she stopped and turned. *Those two are fixed, right?*

Snacks just shrugged, the question beyond his scope. It would not be until later that afternoon, when while washing Snacks' dishes, Angie would look outside and see the answer to her question--occurring in vigorous and very messy fashion, right on her new lawn chairs.

Jack and Angie took well to their new identity as a dog family. They went out and bought sweaters for these pups, fancy new beds, sports-themed tags, and the like. One of their favorite new activities became walking the trio together on the local path, saying hello to all the fellow pet-lovers, and sparking up conversations about the blessed lifestyle that was caring for canines. Most of their down time was spent by the pool, sitting with the dogs encircling them as they read or simply sat back and enjoyed the sun.

Snacks was surprisingly responsible when it came to caring for the dogs. He fed them twice daily, washed them as needed, and Angie would swear that these dogs didn't poop, because she never found any evidence to prove her wrong. Still, Angie was very cautious when admiring her tenant because he always seemed to have a cavalcade of uses for his "kind acts". The trash cans were still filled beyond capacity, the dishes still stacked up in the sink, and of course, he still had not paid one dime of rent.

As one might have guessed, it was more about the psychological torture that Snacks had waged against Angela than anything he had actually done. Angie would rack her brain at how annoying he was with his loud music, his constant opening/beeping/slamming of the microwave, and the way he would bend all her spoons because he was too impatient to wait for his ice cream to thaw, but these weren't capital offenses. True, she shouldn't have to endure anything she didn't want in her own home, but at the same time, she felt that she was being prissy. It was this constant torment of judging herself that really made it so damn hard to live with this man. In fact, if she were being truly honest with herself, she wouldn't even be hung up on things like rent if he was forthcoming and open about it, instead of being wily and sneaky in his attempts to avoid contributing. If he kept the house in order, and he was neither seen nor heard, she'd probably never even bring it up.

65

And now, he actually had her preemptively stopping herself from asking him to do anything! Angie thought to herself that if she went to him right now and asked him to pay his agreed-upon rent, he could and probably would explain that he spends a good amount--maybe $100 to $250--on the dogs' food and basic needs. When you add the labor of walking them, feeding them, plus the other maintenance like fixing broken drawers and trimming the trees, it pretty much added up to the rent. This is exactly why she didn't want to get into this arrangement, but somehow he had maneuvered it this way nonetheless. She didn't see it coming, and couldn't stop it while it was happening, but now there was literally no way she could ever start the process to kick him out. Any way she put it, he had a defense where she would look like a brat who was just whining because she wanted things her way and only her way.

There was one alternative, but it required a little more thought than being a last ditch effort to remove her tenant. In addition, she would really like to be married before this happened, and that was an entirely different issue. So, for the time being, she was stuck. She had decided that it would be best to just endure. Put her head down and get through the trials without letting them get to her. She would focus on how little these annoyances were and how infantesimal they were in comparison to the horrors occurring all across the world. Patience was the key. In no time at all, Jack would ask her to marry him. That might even be the change that makes Snacks realize he should vacate, but probably not. No, she would need to wait a bit longer until she convinced Jack to have children, then finally act upon it.

Yes, it would not be long before she would have her children running around the house and there would only be people tied to her by blood and direct-marriage occupying her living space. These future moments would all be worth these current struggles, just as her past struggles had led to some of the best parts about her current moments. There was a way in which everyone could win and Angie was determined to achieve just this. She would get her home to herself, Jack would avoid forcing his eldest brother back into a world in which he was in no way equipped to survive, and Snacks would have the opportunity to finally grow up. This was exactly how perfect the universe was supposed to work.

Angie knew she was lucky in how she was able to see so much of the bigger picture, and how she had the wisdom to do so even under her current levels of stress. She prided herself on her ability to solve problems with the tact to leave everyone happy. Of course, this need to be loved by everyone all the time was exactly what got her into this trouble in the first place, and it was delaying her significantly at present, but none of that would matter if she could get what she needed to get done in a somewhat swift fashion. The sooner the better, and of course, she wouldn't have it any other way.

MEMORIAL DAY

Jack wasn't the baby of the family, but he might as well have been. The only brother younger than him was of course the black sheep Stanley. This was in fact something Stanley cherished very much, because much like Angie, he found most of the family tendencies worthy of a few slams of the forehead to the drywall. In fact, it was really unfortunate that Stanley was never around because as their brief correspondence had shown, he and Angie would have gotten along famously and perhaps would have even provided the other with an empathetic bounce board for various issues with the boys. Anyway, since Stanley always left a bit of distance between him and his brothers, Jack became the de facto baby, and was forced to assume that role's responsibilities and torments.

The household that Mama Norossi ran was already a circus, but the lax attitude of her husband--known as Bobz (even to his sons)--did not help. To put it simply, the house was anarchy--think 18th Century France, but everyone liked Marie Antoinette. Mama pretty much left the policing to the children, which may have been her intention as in shoving responsibility upon them to hasten their maturity, but anyone who has even read the back cover of *The Lord of the Flies* knows that was a bad premise with which to raise young men. This itself was probably the key error. Had she birthed even one girl, she might have seen differently, but with a gang of boys, she figured they would pretty much raise themselves. Of course, what ended up happening was that the older boys became dictators and the younger ones were forced to fall in line. Like most American school systems or penitentiaries, the bigger, older kids made the real rules, but unlike schools and jails, in the Norossi home, if they needed a superior's blessing to continue their reign, it was obtained with little to no resistance.

Jack's childhood was not one that had him reporting to Mama or Bobz, but rather to Snacks, Stevey, and to an extent, Isaac--this was a case where his strong build outranked his younger age. Snacks was the ganglord, with Isaac as his main muscle and Stevey as more of the diplomatic wing of the Reich. Of course, this meant that Paul, Jackson, and Stanley were at the mercy of the other three at any given moment.

As with most anarchistic political systems, there was a cease-fire that had been achieved, but it was not a stasis that was appreciated by the lowest tier, known from this point on as The Bottom Feeders. The controlling party, known as the Triumvirate, literally never completed a chore, washed a dish, or shared any toy. The Bottom Feeders were quickly indoctrinated to fill these roles lest they feel the wrath of noogies, gut punches, or if Isaac was really pissed, a double wet willy.

Now, Mama Norossi might have been a mediocre parent, but she was no fool. She knew her sons' arrangement, and from time to time, she would reprimand her beloved Snacks for bullying his brothers. These were the very rare occasions where she reminded him of his responsibility as the oldest brother. In hindsight, she would have been better off snapping at Stevey and asking him to enact the change, because all Snacks did was nod, smile, tell his mother how much he loved her and how he would like to apologize on behalf of his siblings... then proceed to give each of the little brothers three gut punches for either ratting or being so sloppy that their mom noticed their anguish.

It really is quite interesting how much one's childhood impacts one's adulthood, even in instances of light trauma such as this. By that same token, it's also a damn shame that one doesn't get much control of one's childhood and thus we are all resigned to enter our adult years with the potentially toxic and self-defeating tendencies that were formed when we were at the mercy of our parents and the many other imperfect adults tasked with looking after us.

See, all of these boys were shaped by this arrangement. In a sort of lasting Stockholm effect, these grown men still fear Snacks as much as they did when they were boys. Of course, now they don't necessarily think they'll get punched in the gut if they cross him, but that lingering intimidation will likely remain ad infinitum. In the same way, the Bottom Feeders are still today considered weak and at a lower social level--at least in the Triumvirate's eyes. This makes no sense now because Jack is a very successful marketing account man, Paul makes a healthy living as a car salesman, and Stanley is one of the most successful wine and food critics in South Beach. Snacks is... well, you know. Isaac is (still) unemployed, and Stevey lives a decent life as a high school teacher, but his wife, daughter, and probably soon his grandchild, walk all over him in embarrassing fashion. Meanwhile, Mama Norossi and Bobz still brag about all of them equally to all their friends. For some--honestly admirable at this point--reason, she always leads off by talking about her precious Snacks.

It goes without saying that Angie did not know this about the boys when she met Jack, and she was just now starting to see this dynamic unfold. This was only natural, because as the weakest of the bunch, Jack was not too inclined to talk about his brothers or his childhood, especially with regards to them. He also did his best to avoid having too many of the Triumvirate together because they would end up reverting to their old roles and gang up on him. So, Angie had met these boys and spoken with them, sure, but she had no idea who the Norrossi clan really was.

Thanks to the perfect nature of this universe, she was about to get a clinic in their family dynamics at the upcoming Memorial Day BBQ. For the first time in their relationship and for the first time in the new house, she would see all the Norossis together, from Mama to maybe even Stanley. Angie just hoped that she was ready, but in truth, no one could possibly be ready for what her own family would later refer to as NorossiMania.

•••

Although Angie would have selected essentially the same guest list, it was actually Snacks who invited everyone over. When she tried to confront him about how it was not polite to invite people over to someone else's home, he countered by saying that Isaac had invited himself and he was the one telling everyone about it. Since Jack didn't say anything, he thought it was cool to do the same. Despite that minor annoyance, she was very much looking forward to having not only her boyfriend's family over, but together with her own family. She was indeed apprehensive about how her highly judgmental mother and sisters would take to the loud and proud Norossis, but she figured she would marry into them soon enough, so they better just get used to it now.

She would never admit this, but the BBQ was also a good opportunity for her to show her family that she was just as stable and settled down as they were. Since both her sisters were married and had children, Angie felt she really needed to hammer it home to her traditional mother that her current situation was just as "grown up" as the other two. True, she didn't have a ceremony or even a ring to prove it, but she was by all accounts married. She was a homeowner and she even had pets. If one wanted to be cheeky about it, Snacks was pretty much their kid at this point, too.

Something that Angie would admit to was that she personally felt like she always needed to work harder to impress her mother. This was mostly a product of being the youngest in the family and like Jack, perpetually sentenced to being seen as a "baby". Add to this that Angie was pretty much the black sheep of her family in how she was more unbridled in her emotions and loved to travel and meet new people, and one can see how her mother would look upon these habits without much appreciation. However, she had accrued many impressive contacts, conversation starters, and a very respectable career in sports entertainment. Thus, there was really nothing for her to prove. In fact, the sad truth was that her mother had only one way of determining whether a woman was successful, and it was something that needed marriage to precede it to count. Angie decided a long time ago that she did not necessarily want children at a young age as was the custom, and she was ready to deal with her mother's judgments accordingly. She instead concerned herself with the (unattainable) task of impressing her mother with her other lofty accomplishments. It should be obvious that she would never see it this way, but every time Angie needed to give a little extra sweat to a job, she thought about how the success of it would look to her mother, and as faulty as the logic may have been, she had succeeded in building a very nice life with this technique.

Despite the lingering mommy/daddy issues in both, one could not deny that perhaps the couple's greatest area of compatibility was in how much they valued their families. Blood was very much thicker than water to the two, and thus, they could not wait to start the process of making the Norossis and the Saccomannos one in the same. Both had very much anticipated the moment when they could combine their loved ones with the other's, and on Memorial Day, they would get their first chance. If the fates saw fit, the gathering would not be forgotten anytime soon.

The first issue with the Memorial Day BBQ should have been obvious, but as is often the case with blatant signs like this one, it wasn't. Jack and Angie were going on six years of dating, and over one full year of living together in a home they both owned. Now, this was not 1970. It was common for people to move-in together at almost any stage of a relationship and many couples cohabitated for a number of years without feeling the need to get the government involved. However, it was a bit of an issue when Angie considered the fact that they had already signed an agreement that was literally going to take thirty years to fulfill.

Thirty years was of course less than a lifetime, if they would be so lucky, but it was still quite a commitment. It was only natural that she felt as if Jack should have proposed either before or right after that mortgage was enacted. Truth be told, she was expecting it every date from the moment they made the offer. Looking back, she felt so embarrassed about that expectation that she buried it as deeply as she possibly could and began the process of convincing herself that she didn't need to get married, and that this situation could stay just as it was "Til Death" and that would be absolutely lovely.

However, this mindset slowly eroded as time was added to the equation. To be clear, it wasn't like she feared Jack would all of a sudden abandon her. Nor was she suspicious of his reluctance to lock her down as being a sign of immaturity. It was closer to her love for the traditional narrative of being a "married" woman.

Although she was the defector of the Saccomannos, she was still a victim to one of their signature qualities in how much they loved traditionalism. Angie managed to escape norms like becoming a housewife or being a shy woman who was supposed to wait for a man to make the first move, but she was dead to rights when it came to the three traditional aspects of being an adult: buying a home, getting married, and having children.

The traditional aspect was a major problem, because without it, Angie would have just asked him to marry her. There was no reason she shouldn't. She had considered it for a short while and she found no logical reason as to why she should sit around and wait for something to happen when she could hasten it herself. However, her logic was not sufficient to force her hand, and she finally realized the harsh truth that she could never pull that trigger and forever tell the story (especially to her mother) of how she had to spearhead the wedding because she couldn't count on her husband to do so.

The BBQ was bringing these issues up because it was a family gathering with the massive missing element of the host couple being "legitimate" family. The makeup of this household was definitely not what she had imagined and that was fine, but as it became more obvious that the stasis achieved would remain static for an indeterminable amount of time, the rate of her sleepless nights increased. It was getting so bad that she was starting to fantasize about Jack proposing to her at the BBQ itself, when she knew very well that she would sooner see Snacks move out of her house and present her with all the back-rent before that happened.

Speaking of the devil, Jack's brother had recently found a new way to irk his potential sister-in-law. He had always made it a habit of leaving his food in the microwave. Snacks never cooked. (It was likely that he had no idea how food was even made.) Instead, he ordered out every single meal, except for his "snacks" like chips, Twinkies, and such that he bought from the corner store. Every single night without fail, he would walk in with his styrofoam take-out box and either directly store it into the microwave, or toss it right into the kitchen trash. This made no sense at all because the garage is right next to the big trash can. One must literally walk past that bin to get into the house, but Snacks still regularly would toss his scraps into the trash in the kitchen, vastly limiting its capacity until Angie or Jack had to take it right back outside. Of course Snacks never once took out the trash, which Angie finally figured is why he didn't understand how stupid it was for him to do any of this in the first place. She even began to believe that he didn't understand that the big bin was how trash left the house.

Angie had somewhat come to peace with that habit, but now he was upping the ante. Snacks must have somehow heard or figured out that it was cheaper to just eat extra large pizzas for dinner the majority of the week. He would often leave the house at 21:00 or later to pick up a pizza and upon his return, he would open the box and start eating the slices right out of it. This was surprisingly green of him, even though it can be assured that he only did this because grabbing a plate was far too much work.

When he finished that first night's serving, he found himself with a storage problem since an extra large pizza box had no place in a microwave, and it couldn't even fit in the fridge. Snacks certainly was not going to divide the pieces into some kind of plastic container, so he strategized a better solution where he just tossed the entire pizza box into the oven. This was totally fine for everyone involved since it didn't interfere with Jack or Angie's use of the kitchen--that is, until it did.

There was a Saccomanno tradition of baking excellence and it had all but missed Angie. While her mother was a master of confection and her sisters had their respective talents, Angie was too much of a loose cannon to follow the generational recipes and she would often overpower them with too much sugar and butter. Determined to fix this and to do so in grand fashion with the debut of a classic apple pie at the Memorial Day BBQ, she used the preceding weeks to practice. She dug up the old recipe, did some research on the side to compare, and finally created a gameplan to create at least three practice pies before the official one was disseminated.

She managed to get the first pie to a decent level by keeping EXACTLY to the specifications handed down to her mother from her mother and so on up the line. Naturally, this was not good enough for Angie and she made her own notes on the formula accordingly. She estimated that by swapping out a certain breed of apples and by opting for a more natural type of sugar, she could improve it. With the improvements noted, she scheduled attempt number two for that weekend.

Always pressed for time, Angie arrived home that day with her fresh ingredients and quickly began chopping them up as required. Of course, she had no idea that the night before, Snacks had brought home one of his extra large pizza pies and promptly stored the cardboard box with its remains in the oven. After hurrying around the kitchen and finishing up the prep, she took a beat to relax, knowing that she had some down time while the oven warmed up. So, she simply set it to 375 and walked away.

Normally, Angie was very anti-nap. Instead, she liked to lie on her bed with her eyes closed and embark on a sort of light meditation where she simply cleared her mind of all stimulation and let her mental recover. She had planned to do just this for about fifteen or so minutes until her oven was ready to proceed. As she lied there, her mind wandered a bit thinking about the party and her should-be husband. She thought about Snacks and how he would react to their marriage. Would he be pissed? Would he go so far as to sabotage it? Has he been talking to Jack about it and advising him not to take the plunge? This line of thinking had become extreme by this point, so she worked to clear her entire head once more. As she focused on her deep breathing, she thought that it was working counterintuitively because she actually began to smell what she thought was a BBQ. However, the smell of contained fire relaxed her immensely and she began to reflect on the good times to be had at their own big shindig. Surely, the Norossis and the Saccomannos would have a grand old time and it would spark a tradition of her own. Yes, that would be the perfect ending: setting the precedent for an annual BBQ at their home as a kickoff to the good times to be had all summer.

In no time at all, there would be kids in the pool, her mother would introduce new taste buds to her fantastic antipasto, and Jack would man the grill like the king of his castle. These thoughts filled Angie with an unrivaled warmth and bliss. In fact, she became so relaxed that she began to drift into a light sleep, flirting with falling into a nap.

Fortunately, she was jolted awake by the increasing smell of what she now thought had to be the neighbor's grill. She arose and figured that she should get back to the pie, but maybe first see what her neighbors had cooking, if for nothing else, a little extra menu inspiration. She exited her room into the backyard and peeped over. There was no one in the backs of either homes curiously enough and she concluded that the smokey scent must be from a house further out, despite its pungency. It was not until she entered her own kitchen that she found the root of the smell.

To her horror, the oven was gently letting out a small gray trail of smoke. In another mistake, she approached it and cracked the door, which let out a huge plume of dark cloud that almost blinded her immediately. She stumbled backwards and ran into the closet to grab the fire extinguisher, then headed back into the kitchen and unloaded that sucker as best as she could, drenching the flames in chemical retardant until they were completely quenched. Once the smoke had faded and she was able to open her eyes in the house again, she looked into the oven to see what happened and that is when she found Snacks' pizza box, or at least what was left of it.

Thankfully, no one was home at the time, because Angie would have been terribly embarrassed at her word choice and the volume at which she projected those words. Only the dogs had to witness the embodiment of her frustration, after which she just sat and breathed to regain her composure and begin the process of cleaning up the disaster. She thought about waiting and making Snacks clean up the mess, thinking she could claim that all is forgiven if his penance was this drole task. However, she immediately realized that this would never work, because he would just take his time getting the job done, possibly working in five-square-inch sessions with full day breaks in between. Even if he did act quickly, there would no doubt be tons of leftover chemicals and ash that could realistically poison her or Jack. So, she just cleaned it herself, spending the hours brainstorming ways she could use this very dangerous situation to make progress in getting Snacks the hell out of her house.

Perpetually in the right place at the right time, Snacks arrived home before Jack that evening, robbing Angie of the opportunity to vent before she confronted the culprit. If she hadn't have just come moments away from burning down her lovely home, she might have found it funny that he entered the house holding a fresh pizza box. He placed it down on the kitchen table and said his hello's, before complimenting on how nice the kitchen smelled. Again, this would be hilarious in almost any other circumstance.

Did you leave that pizza box in the oven? she asked as calm as she could, but angry enough that Snacks immediately softened his own tone.

Yeah. You're always welcome to a slice, he said as he took a piece out and chomped into it.

I didn't know you were doing that so I turned it on and your big ass pizza box caught on fire. The whole house almost went up.

Oh shit. Are you okay? he added in between obnoxious chews.

Yes. I'm fine, but if I didn't catch it when I did, the house could've burned down. It's common knowledge that you can't put flammable stuff like that in an oven. You shouldn't even be leaving food out like that anyway. We could get rats or something.

Snacks paused for a moment, seeming to contemplate his egregious lack of judgment and its nearly colossal consequences--at least that's what Angie hoped. He put his pizza slice down and asked, *You didn't check inside before you turned it on?*

Snacks had dodged many bullets in his lifetime, many more than he should have, but that moment could have been the most impressive dodge of his life. He would manage to make it all the way to the end of his life without ever knowing how close he was to it ending right then and there. Angela was within reaching distance of her very expensive and very sharp blade set and her saintly suppression of this man's actions had hit its boiling point. She could have quite easily grabbed a knife and struck down the oldest Norossi brother in the blink of an eye, and Lord knows she had wanted to do just that. Luckily for him, she opted instead to reach for that beautiful chestnut hair of hers, and tug with excessive force as she screamed:

NO, I DIDN'T CHECK MY OWN DAMN OVEN BEFORE I USED IT! No one in this house cooks or bakes. No one even uses the kitchen outside of the microwave. All you guys do is stuff my cabinets with your junk food, pack the fridge with take-out containers, and leave all that shit in the microwave. I would maybe get away with thinking that nothing was used, but you leave such a huge mess everywhere you trot in this house that I have blatant evidence in the form of Spaghetti-O's and dried up cheese to prove that you've been where you've been. Just like those damn boxes you left in the living room for like six months until I had to take time out of my day to move them for you. So, no, I didn't check the oven. Why, in any scenario, would I stop to check inside it before I used it?

Naturally, Snacks was taken aback by the explosion. Of course, he still didn't understand what he did wrong, but he immediately apologized anyway. He figured correctly that the apology alone was not going to be enough to calm Angie's wrath. Instead of defending his

81

position or wielding an excuse, he felt the strongest move would be to just stay as quiet as possible and let her get it all out.

Angie continued: *It's not just that. First of all you agreed to pay us rent to stay here. It's not a huge deal, but you are using water, electricity, wifi, cable, and everything else. You've never paid that. In fact, I told Jack that Isaac couldn't move in since he was unemployed because I didn't want to deal with anyone trying to skip out on what they owed. I don't care about the past, but you need to be paying us that $500 on the first from now on.*

She took a beat to calm a bit, then continued: *You also need to be a little cleaner. Like, wipe down a counter if you spill something on it. Toss your dishes in the dishwasher. Take out the trash if you see it's full. I know you take good care of the dogs and we appreciate it, but we all do a lot. We all live here and we need to take care of our house together.*

When she would tell this story years from now, she would cite her use of the word "our" as her biggest mistake.

Contrary to what Angie believed, Snacks knew very well that she preferred he lived somewhere else. He was not offended or hurt by this fact, but he also knew that as co-owner of the home, his brother had a strong say in who lived there, so he would not give up this place simply because it was her preference. Sure, he was aware that there were times where he could have been more helpful around the household, but he was completely ignorant of his annoying ticks and like most all-star manipulators, that he was even manipulating at all. He had only ever lived with his brothers who never dared to voice their concerns, which deprived him of a chance to address these shortcomings. He also knew he owed rent to the owners, but in true Snacks' fashion he was trying to see how far he could get without paying it. After all, $500 is $500.

Once more, Angie said, *I don't want to yell at you like a child. It's just that we need to do our parts, you know? Jack likes having you here and that's fine, but you can't just hang out and expect us to do all the work that it takes to keep this place from looking like Baghdad.* She stopped there very wisely and avoided complaining about things like how he constantly went in and out of his room all night, how he slammed the microwave door, and how he sometimes parks his car a little too far left so that she has to get out through her passenger door. She also conveniently left out the fact that Jack didn't do dishes or clean the counters, either. Of course, Jack was paying half the mortgage so those circumstances were different, but still.

Snacks picked up on the shift in Angie's energy as she got this load off her chest. He saw her shoulders drop from their hiked position and the flush disappear from her forehead. She didn't speak for a beat, so he jumped in.

I know I don't pull my weight around here as often as I should. Back when it was just Jack and the other two, we kind of just cleaned whenever, and that place was much smaller. I'm not making an excuse. I'll work on it from now on. I'm serious. He gauged Angie from here and saw that she was taking it to heart. *I'm glad you're telling me too because, like you said, I got lots of stuff going on, especially right now with this damn UTI--been to the doctor three times the past two weeks--but anyway, I get swept up with stuff and forget what I should be doing. Don't be afraid to call me on it. Really.*

Thanks, Angie replied warmly. She had been in a bit of a daze since going off, surprising herself with how much she had been holding back over this first year. Was it really as easy as just letting him know what he did wrong? She was not necessarily this foolish, but she was foolish enough to believe that maybe there was a sliver of hope that these two could co-exist.

And I'll get you the rent on Friday, Snacks said as he took his pizza box to his room, giving Angie some long-awaited peace. The final promise was a nice touch, but she was not going to celebrate until she had the check--well, Snacks probably didn't have a bank account, so probably the cash--was in her hands. However, she did her best to remain positive. They had just made some serious progress together and they didn't need the mediation of Jack to do it. Yes, things were improving and you can't go broke making a profit. Angie still wanted Snacks out of that house, and she still wanted to clean up after babies of her own in his place at some point in the near future, but patience was the key. Well, that and making sure that Snacks coughs up his half a grand on Friday.

By Wednesday, even Jack had commented on how much Snacks had changed his tune. He texted Angie and even sent a picture as proof. Snacks was taking out the trash! And he put in a new bag, too! When she got home from work, she gambled by opening the microwave, and nothing was inside. Not only that, it was relatively clean.

Angie was very pleased with these changes, but she was slow to remark on them. She figured that Jack probably expressed his thanks and she did not want to give Snacks the impression that she was letting her guard down just because he did his normal and expected household duties.

Of course, Snacks was a little put off by the fact that after one day and completing a total of two chores, there were no plans for a parade on his behalf. He did not stop to think this deeply about it, but he must have really liked Angie, because this was the most work he had ever done to appease someone. Maybe he just really liked this living arrangement, be it the house, the location, the people, the dogs, or most likely, the combination of it all. Snacks found himself going out of his way--already a first--to keep his landlords happy and avoid another explosion from his brother's girlfriend who he was slowly, but surely starting to respect a great deal. There would be no use in asking him why he was feeling this way, but one might guess that it was because she confronted him. He couldn't remember the last time this had happened. Snacks had coasted through his life with his charm, intimidation, and manipulation skills without ever meeting any serious resistance, and if he did, he would just retreat and find another, easier path. He was slow to realize this, but right now, he was stuck. He couldn't afford to move to a new place, his cousin was living with his girlfriend, and his brother Isaac was broke and sleeping on a rotating list of friends' couches. If Angie insisted, like really insisted, Jack might very well choose her over him.

What would he do then? His only recourse would be to stay with his dad in the trailer home, but his brother Paul and his longtime girlfriend already occupied the living room there. He could probably reclaim that territory, but it would be tight and uncomfortable anyway he looked at it. Angie had really done it. She had not only steered clear of Snacks' traps, but now she had officially boxed him into a trap of her own. This was without a doubt the root of his growing respect for her.

Snacks had waited in the kitchen that night for Angie to get home. He had a rag in his hand so that when she walked in, he could begin wiping down a counter and be "caught in the act". She walked in, lugging her oversized briefcases, and said hello to him, being careful not to give him the satisfaction of mentioning his cleaning. She was not suspicious of his new outlook and dedication to being a decent tenant, but she was certainly not going to gush over what should have been normal. Instead she started the conversation by talking about a favorite subject of hers: how bad the Angels were playing as of late. Snacks played along for a bit, then got right into the meat:

I was gonna tell you to just let me know if there's anything you need before the BBQ, like house-wise.

Angie thought for a bit about the list of about eight hundred tasks that needed to be completed before then, and simplified it into the dozen or so that Snacks could handle. There was cleaning all the outside windows, but he would leave them streaky. There was also shampooing the couches, but that was probably better left to a professional. He would already give the dogs their baths. The only thing she could think for him to do would be to set up the outdoor speakers that she was originally planning on having installed by the retailer. She hadn't thought about it until now, but Snacks worked with sound systems often at his job and could probably do this himself, at a discounted rate, no doubt. So, she asked if he would be interested in the challenge and he immediately responded affirmatively. And just like that, he had earned his first sincere *Thanks* from the tough, but fair Angela Saccomanno.

Sure enough, Snacks installed the system, right away in fact. That Thursday evening, he sat in the backyard waiting for Angie to get home just to start blasting some early hits from The Strokes to surprise her. She heard the music inside the garage and stepped out into the back with a look of impression that Snacks had never seen. This alone was worth the labor. She dropped her heavy bags and took a seat at the table to just sit and groove to the music.

Snacks, this is awesome! she conceded

Yeah, I set it up so you get a nice surround sound right here, and I got some of the smaller ones right by the fire pit for when you're winding down. It's all on bluetooth, so I can hook up your phone, or there's also the AUX in case anyone wants to play something on their device real fast. I talked with Marty, the main guy in Home Audio, and he gave me all these like top end connectors and tons of advice on speaker placement, too.

Incredible, she replied with her eyes closed, getting lost in the newly-shuffled Daft Punk tune.

This is like a $5,000 system with how it performs. No one has anything like this in the city.

You're the best, man.

It really is amazing how one can learn so much about themselves all throughout life's journey. It's also baffling how we're taught to believe that we should know ourselves and lock in personalities in adolescence or even early adulthood.

Snacks had always believed that he was a rebel and a maverick, answering to no one and caring not one speck about another person's opinion, yet with those four words from Angie, he had felt a warmness in his gut that was oh so foreign. Had he really never been complimented before? That couldn't be true, but hearing it just now from Angie certainly felt like the first authentic time that he had been admired for his work. Maybe that was it. It would be impossible to be praised for hard work when one had never actually worked hard. Any way he looked at, Snacks was glad this had happened the way it did, and even though it took a day of his life that he would never get back, the value was unrivaled.

As for Angie, she was in heaven. Not only was this sound system just what she had always wanted, but it existed in a home that she owned, and on top of that it was installed by what had been the biggest thorn in her side for almost a year. She was a few weeks away from hosting her BBQ and things were looking very much up. This was actually her life now, and she loved it. She had the man of her dreams, her dream job, and her dream home. Lying back in her chair with that French duo's serene electro beats playing, she could only think to herself how she wanted to keep "sleeping" forever.

Of course, that would be impossible and an alarm would unfortunately sound that very next day.

Angie was actually not miserable on the drive home that following evening. Despite the agonizing Friday traffic, her mindset was locked on the positives. She refused to think about how Snacks might weasel out of his rent tonight, or how he might regress at any given moment. She gave the universe her good thoughts of how she would come home and see a nice stack of cash on the table, poetically in opposition to that cursed stack of boxes that haunted the living room so many months ago. As a matte black Tesla blatantly cut her off to gain position in her just-starting-to-move lane, she just turned up her sports talk podcast and brushed it right off. No one had the power to ruin her weekend mood.

She pulled into her garage, parked the vehicle, and stepped out, making the call to leave her bags in the car since it was Friday and she would not need to worry about them for two long days. There was no music playing tonight, but there was noise coming from inside the house. Jack had texted her that he would be working from home today, so she figured it was just him shuffling around. As she approached the door, she heard Snacks' voice, too, expletives in fact. He was angry, but he wasn't

87

directing it at Jack. She walked into the house and drew everyone's attention.

Hey guys, she said as she identified the intense vibe of the room. *What's wrong?*

Jack looked over at Snacks to let him take the lead. He shook his head and avoided eye contact with his landlord. *I lost my damn job. Fucking assholes.* Snacks almost looked like he was about to cry. Upon hearing the news, Angie almost wept herself.

What happened? she asked, withholding judgment as best as she could.

They said things are slowing down and they needed to cut hours. It all got really ugly fast because you know a lot of those guys are barely making it with what they pay now. I was safe, but I had to stand up for the guys that weren't. I told them this was bullshit and that we worked too hard to get bent over like this. We all lost our heads and said some things we probably shouldn't have, but they went and called in security and that's when I went off. Who the hell calls security on their own employees? Be a leader. This isn't a… a… dictatorship. I told everyone to calm down and asked the dude to just cut some of my hours, and the other managers agreed. The rep told us that they couldn't do that because they needed us, and I told them to piss off. I said either give us a better solution or I'm walking.

Upon hearing where this was going, Angie's heart sank.

He continued: *They wouldn't budge, so I walked right out of the meeting. Two other managers and all the part-timers followed me. Let 'em try to sell speakers and TV's and shit now.*

So you didn't officially quit? she asked in a level of desperation with which she was most definitely not familiar.

Well, they're not gonna take me back after I walked half the damn staff out of there. Shit, even if they offered me a raise, I'd say no. That place has been getting worse and worse every day for years. It probably won't even be standing in another six months.

Angie was very careful not to explode at this point. She managed to suppress the urge to scream at Snacks that his employer was the biggest electronics retailer in the country and had no chance of folding anytime within the next five to ten years, at least. She refused to immediately bring up her inquiry as to how he was planning to pay rent now, and how it is mighty convenient that this new development happened on the exact day he promised to pay his first installment. She instead internalized her energy and filtered out the sharp bits to continue with:

I understand. They can't expect you to muscle out other employees. They're obviously trying to make management the bad guys instead of taking the heat themselves. I get that. I'm just wondering if they'll come to their senses after what you did. Maybe you just need to give them a few days. I mean, they'll probably reach out to you and then you can go in there and find a way to compromise.

Snacks just shook his head and took a seat, obviously flustered beyond rational thought. Jack added: *Don't worry about it anymore. They'll either reach out or not. Take a day or something to just relax and you can look for a new job after that.*

Thanks, Jack. And Angie. I'm... I'm fucking embarrassed. He suddenly stood up and made a step toward his room. *I'm getting you that rent money.*

Snacks, Angie said, stopping him. She was not sure why she did this--especially after spending over a full year trying to get him to do the exact opposite--but she did. She took a good long look at Raphael Norossi, a grown man of over 50 that answered to a child's nickname. Truly, he was a man in stature only. He couldn't readily keep a roof over his head. He couldn't sustain any relationship that wasn't bound by blood. He could barely feed himself. And now, he couldn't even hold down a job. What was he going to do if they abandoned him? What would he have done if she and Jack had moved into a one bedroom apartment? In that brief moment, she saw--behind all of his quirks and personality flaws--just a helpless little boy. He had been so good at hiding his fears and insecurities, but right now, he had no more defense. She had taken in a scared child, who only had his job to prove that he contributed to society in any way. Now that job was gone, because he had sacrificed it for his underlings. All of this flooded her head at once and she finally let out:

If you don't get your job back, I'm sure you'll get another one real soon. You have to. I'm serious. You can't live here without a job, because you need to pay rent. For now, just focus on figuring this out. She swallowed deeply before finally adding: *You don't need to worry about paying us this month.*

Snacks avoided all eyes, looking down. On one hand he was off the hook, but on the other hand, he would have to verbally accept this charity from his brother. Part of him even believed that this was Angie's entire plan. No doubt she picked up on the power dynamics by now and she's clearly been active in trying to control him. It wouldn't be far off to discern that it would be extra sweet for her to hear him accept that his brother was more successful than him, so much so that he needed to be a parasite just to survive.

Fortunately for Snacks, he never thought deeply about anything. So, he looked up at Angie, then at his brother and simply said: *Okay. Thank you, but I'm getting you guys dinner tonight. Don't fight me on it.*

With smiles all around, Snacks headed into his room. Jack reluctantly peeked over at his girlfriend, hoping that her glare would not be too intense. He was disappointed. Her look was so fierce, no words were needed. Although today she was understanding and cordial, by June 1st, if Snacks was still without a means to pay his rent, it would be war.

...

Angie's oldest sister, Berenice, didn't work and thus had the freedom to engage in many time-consuming hobbies. One of these included her god-given knack for storytelling. Although she started her career early on as an orator with a flashlight under her chin for theatrics, Bee found a way to channel this early penchant into a more lucrative means by writing paperbacks, which she could afford to publish thanks to her very successful entrepreneur husband. It's not that these books were terrible, they were just all the exact same story with a piece or two swapped. Essentially, they told of a beautiful young woman who was always underestimated by those around her, and she eventually surprises everyone with acts of heroism and intellectual prowess in some way or another and everyone is in awe of the fact that the protagonist is both gorgeous and capable. If one was rather unkind, he or she might call these books a perpetual fantasy-fulfillment for the unfulfilled writer, but they kept her busy and she managed to cultivate a small audience who enjoyed them.

Berenice tried to write as much as possible, and this included letters to her mother and sisters. She also wrote to her in-laws, but they almost never wrote back. Instead, they would send a text to say they received the letter and that it was good to hear from her. Bee feared that they weren't even being read, but that truth would hurt too much, so she never tested it.

Angie adored her sister's letters and oftentimes, her whole day brightened when she saw one of those fancy envelopes on the table awaiting her after a long day at work. This is exactly what happened on this day, when she saw a fresh arrival with that trademark whale sticker on the seal. Angie carefully opened the letter and began to read:

Dear Angie,

I am so excited to see you guys in a few weeks! Thank you for inviting us all to your beautiful home. Memorial Day is a very special holiday and it is so very important for us to spend it with our families as we appreciate the freedoms and privileges that so many soldiers have died to protect. I know you understand this and I thank you for being so proactive in celebrating this honor.

Ariana has been looking forward to the party so much that we just went out and got her a new swimsuit, and she has been modeling it for us everyday. She keeps saying how she wants to show her Auntie Angie how fast she can swim now, so I hope you clear time to appreciate her progress. I have also confirmed that Todd will be coming with us. He said he absolutely must see your new house, so he moved his schedule around and made it so that he'll have the whole weekend to spend with us.

I'm sure you've spoken with Charlie, but she has been telling me that she will be a little late because Keegan has a hockey tournament in the morning. (She has also hinted at the fact that his team is not quite ready for intense competition, so they will probably only be a bit late if that is an accurate statement.) You can rest assured that her boys will put that pool to use. I just hope that Oscar can keep them from getting too crazy, even though I just love seeing them scurry around like they always do. It reminds me of Charlie when she was their age. Mama would always tell me to wrangle her in and I'd get so nervous that I wouldn't be able to. Anyway, please advise both of us on what you would like us to bring, too. You can mark me down for the fruit spread, but if there is anything else, do not hesitate to ask.

Now, I do need to give you a little information on Mama. There is nothing to be concerned about, but she has been hinting at an issue that I'm sure you're aware of. You know our mother and how much she values tradition. We love her as she is, but she is as stubborn as a woman could be and we must do our best to honor her despite this shortcoming. I spoke with her recently about the BBQ and she has alluded to the fact that she would not be as comfortable as she would like around the Norossi family because you and Jack are not even engaged. I, myself, am very surprised that Mama did not make a big issue of you two moving in together in the first place, knowing her views, but I was happy to see that she did not let those views interfere with her love and support. However, after a year of living with a man, she is… let's say annoyed that he has not married you, much less proposed. This is clearly none of my business, nor is it hers. I simply am relaying what she is probably withholding from you, because you do deserve to know. This goes without saying, but I am always open to discuss or to intercede on your behalf.

In closing, I am very happy to see your life flourishing! You have a beautiful home, a handsome, hard-working, and dedicated lover, and a career where you can show your wide range of skills. I am sure it will not be long before I am bawling my eyes out at your dream wedding, then eventually stealing your children away for an afternoon at the movies. I am counting the days until your big gathering, and as always, please reach out to me if you need anything at all.

With much love,
Bee

•••

Never underestimate the power of boredom. Even someone as lazy and unmotivated as Snacks Norossi often found himself a slave to his boredom and much to the pleasure of both Jack and Angie, it was the impetus that was keeping their house in the best shape it had ever been. The lawn was well manicured, the back was nicely swept, and they never once had to fill an empty paper towel dispenser. On top of this, Snacks had mounted some of their closeted artwork and he had organized all the tools and storage in the garage. This was rather ridiculous because Snacks was doing in a few hours what would normally have taken him months on his normal employed schedule. He didn't realize how hard he was working, of course. He was simply bored out of his mind. Rather than try harder to find a new job, or at least sit and self-examine where his life was at the moment and where he wanted it to go, he just started doing manual labor until enough time passed that he could just go to bed for the night.

Angie certainly didn't complain, but she did worry about the perpetual issue with Snacks: his stasis. She was careful to thank him for his work when she saw what he had completed every day, but she was also cautious that it should be no more than one simple word of gratitude. In addition, she asked him about his job search every day, but in very clever ways. If she went in and ambushed him with the same question day after day, he would very realistically stop the search altogether just to spite her so she had to frame it in ways like mentioning places that were hiring or even remarking on how he had been working so much harder unemployed than he had when he was at the beck and call of a supervisor. He played along and went right into how he was talking to a friend or two about openings and how he would always ask if a place was hiring when he went out. This was okay for now, but Angie worried greatly about how long she would be sheltering a bum and when this would reach a breaking point to where they had to feed and clothe him too.

On this particular day, Snacks approached her first. He was throwing out the trash into the big dumpster--already a sight to behold--when she drove up. She hopped out and he came over to help her with her oversized load of backpacks and briefcases. After the cordials he launched into his pitch:

I was going to tell you... obviously this job search is taking time and I don't know what's going to happen, but since I'm home more now, you can give me a list of any other stuff you need before the BBQ. The sound system's working great and I just wanted to offer up my time since I have so much. That way you don't have anything extra to worry about.

Angie was surprised, but she shoved that reaction deep down and simply replied that his offer was very thoughtful. For some reason, when he proposed his services this time around, she was much more open to his help. Maybe it had something to do with how his behavior and contribution had improved as of late, or maybe it was just because time was running out and she needed as many hands on deck as she could get, but the point stood that she was now more than ready to hand him her long list of duties. However, she was sure to add that he should not sacrifice time toward his job search just to cross off tasks for the BBQ. Snacks said he was surely not thinking of doing that, but in the meantime, it made sense for him to increase his contribution to the house since he could not pay the agreed-upon rent.

Angie headed into her room that night a bit more at ease than she had been since Snacks announced his abdication of his job. She very much hoped he would not get too far into the list before he had to stop because he found a new source of income, but she admitted this was better than nothing. The BBQ was that important to her, and she welcomed any widdling of obstacles in making it the best event it could be.

Her decision to let go of trying to micromanage Snacks into a new job was rewarded tenfold. In the weeks leading up to the BBQ, he completed every single task on her list. He scooped leaves out of the gutters, mopped the floors, scrubbed down the bathrooms, and he picked up some plants and placed them throughout the house accordingly. He also changed water filters, made the reservations for the kegs, washed the dogs, framed some portraits, refilled the fire extinguisher, bought her signature scented candles, changed the welcome mat, touched up the deck paint, and he even stored some clutter.

Angie was not even going to waste the calories thinking about why he was being so flagrantly submissive. His motivations or his long game was completely irrelevant. She didn't even care about the rent at this point. Her house looked gorgeous and she didn't have to sweat and stress to make it so. She had lived with Snacks long enough to know this most definitely had an ulterior motive, but she figured that as long as it happened after the party, she could handle it. Fortunately for her, this was mostly the case.

The day arrived and everything was perfectly in its place. It was a warm day that raised thermometers as soon as the sun made its way over the foothills. That bright beast shone brightly on the Norossi/Saccomanno backyard, and was broken only by the new Snacks-installed awning that shaded the immaculate setting.

Angie woke up extra early and set her favorite music on the outdoor speaker system as she made the final touches to the venue. Since Snacks had done the majority of the labor, she really just needed to make tiny tweaks here and there to ensure the specifications were exact.

She had told her guests to arrive at any time after 13:00, meaning she needed the place ready to entertain at 12:00. By 10:00, she was showered, dressed, and fully made-up. Even Snacks was awake at this point, and he had made an offer to pick up any last minute items for the hosts. The only challenge at this point was waking up Jack. At 11:00, Angie went into their bedroom and saw him crashed the hell out, lying on top of the various sheets and blankets. He had to work the day before because there was a major deadline with a client and since Jack was so vital to that firm, they asked him to come in and oversee some of the project. When she received the text informing her of this, Angie was perturbed. She always felt like they took advantage of Jack, and she was nearly sure that in reality, this was another grunt work task that the other account managers talked themselves out of when approached. Her brow furrowed thinking about how Jack was likely the only one who was not able to back out of the holiday weekend assignment, and at the rate and intensity he worked, he was clearly the most deserving of that break. It was this line of thought that summoned the pity and understanding for her sleepy boyfriend. Otherwise, she would no doubt be screaming at him for slacking on such an important day. However, at this late hour, she had no choice but to force him awake and have him begin to get ready.

After an escalating process that took about fifteen minutes longer than she expected, Jack woke up and sipped the coffee his girlfriend brewed specially for him. He asked if there was anything he needed to do and she told him that his brother had taken care of everything. Jack took a brief moment to rub this in her face, then proceeded to hop into the shower and commence his routine.

Angie spent the next moments making her hors d'oeuvres and clearing her mind for what was sure to be a fun, but nerve-racking day. She thought to herself for a moment about how quickly it would pass, as all memorable times usually do. They would laugh, talk, sing, dance, and just enjoy the fact that the infinite paths of the universe somehow converged in bringing them all together… then it would be over, and they would all wait for the next time they could gather.

Although she had mainly made this such a priority because to her this was going to be the debut of this group of people as one family, she realized that they already were a family. She knew long ago that she was in love with Jack and that she would humbly accept any life that he could give her, because she knew he would give her everything he could. Naturally, she would do the same. She had come from a very small group and she always had the desire to marry into a really big family filled with characters and personalities, the likes of which she had never seen. Some might say to be careful what one wishes for because the Norossis were about as wild and "unique" a clan as one would ever see. However, Angie was wise enough to shift focus from the benefits and problems of the family and instead put that energy into the fact she knew so very well: as long as she had Jack, all would be well.

The only troubling issue that she couldn't shake was how Stanley had never answered his invitation. She was of course worried that she had offended him by speaking so freely about his brother. Sure he seemed to dive into the Snacks slander first, but maybe she went too far. She was still an outsider. For just a moment, she even believed that he might show up just to tell her off to her face. She managed to finally bury this thought by leaving it up to the gods and assuming the most likely explanation: Stanley was simply too busy to answer back. In fact, she could even double up and send him a recap as early as tomorrow, just for her own peace of mind.

Of course, Mama Saccomanno was the first to arrive. She came in by herself with an oversized plate couriering a presentation of her famous antipasto that was so exquisite, it was nearly pornographic. Angie took the dish from her and led her into the house. After the flurry of hugs and kisses that was a Saccomanno standard, she excitedly began showing off the home. Her mother was very impressed with everything she had done with the place since she last visited and she even complimented her on the cleanliness of the space--top praise from someone as surgical as she was in her own cleaning.

When they ended the tour, they headed into the backyard right as the doorbell rang. Angie scurried over and welcomed in her sister Bee with her husband Todd, who was cradling their toddler, Ariana. She led them all into the back to say hello to Mama and then they began their own tour. This cycle continued once again as Charlie arrived with her husband Oscar, and their rambunctious boys.

The Norossis were all late, which allowed for a small Saccomanno gathering to kick things off. During this time, the extended family was able to chat about various subjects from their children to career updates and upcoming vacation plans. This was a nice and unexpected development. Angie had been afraid that while hosting the party she wouldn't have a lot of time to sit with her sisters and mother, but not only had she had this excess, she even had Jack here with her.

Jack and Mama got along famously, which had become a normal sight by now. On their first meeting, Mama took her to the side and told her that he was a good man, which was about the nicest thing she had ever said about the gender as a whole. Of course, this was a massive endorsement for Jack and watching them converse together like two old friends was about the best thing she had ever seen. However, Angie spoiled this moment by overthinking about how Mama was probably laughing and joking, but deep down looking for a reason as to why this man was waiting so long to marry her daughter. She could be noticing his uncalloused hands or his two-day scruff and thinking about how these were signs of a man-child who was adept at wasting time and stringing naive women along until they had their fill. These fears made their way to the forefront when Mama playfully mentioned that Jack and Angie would be more than able to host their wedding reception in this backyard.

Jack skillfully agreed right away, but for some reason thought it made sense to add that his brother would be game to lead that charge, just like he did for this one. Mama of course kept her reaction muted, but everyone still noticed. This was the first clear break in philosophies between the Norossis and the Saccomannos, but no worry was necessary, many more would be upcoming.

An awkward beat passed where Angie later realized she should have just jokingly added that she hoped he wouldn't still be here. This would have most definitely evoked a laugh from her side, and probably a cheap one from Jack as well, who would forget all about it by the time the night was over. Instead, she let the silence creep its ugly head in and hold everyone hostage until Snacks himself emerged from the house.

The perpetual guest said his hello's and met the husbands, generously serving up an annoying joke for each. He remarked on Todd's t-shirt and how it surprised him since he figured rich guys wore tuxes everywhere, then he told Oscar that he knew he was the little hockey players' dad based on how rough his knuckles were. No doubt they had been of use during his own disagreements on the ice. Snacks definitely knew how to charm people, and it was really a sight to behold in how quickly he could get on a stranger's good side even while distributing backhand compliments to them. After a polite beat, he excused himself to check on the dogs, who were sadly residing in the dog run on the side of the home and surely would appreciate the attention.

Todd immediately remarked on how Snacks was a funny guy and he could see why they kept him around, for which he received a fist to the deltoid from his wife. Mama chimed in that the Norossi genes bear handsome men and once more poked the room's elephant by saying that she certainly hoped they would have boys. Right as Jack responded that there hadn't been a girl born to them yet, the doorbell rang. As if on cue, Isaac arrived with his latest flame, Becky, and his father, Bobz. Following right behind them was Paul and his girlfriend Irene.

Angie thought she might have been a tad too critical in the fact that the first thing she noticed was that no one had brought anything. She had to give them the benefit of the doubt that Jack didn't remind them that you absolutely never showed up to a party empty-handed, but the fact still remained that five grown adults thought it would be acceptable to just waltz into a house and start eating and drinking the free stuff.

She gave them all hugs and welcomed them to the home, hoping that no one would ask for a tour--a hope about which she would later feel guilty. Luckily, no one was interested and they all immediately headed to the backyard where they began to find their seats and mingle.

Naturally, the Norossis found a table of their own and a de facto border was created. If one were to get lost at any point, he or she simply needed to look at the tables: the Norossi one was lined with beer bottles, while the Saccomanno was filled with diet soda cans and wine glasses.

Right away, Isaac saw Jack at the Saccomanno table and wrapped him in a headlock. He smiled and played like he was roughhousing, but Jack was clearly uncomfortable and his cheeks rouged darker and darker as he tried to tap out. This was quite the introduction to the most polarizing of Norossi brothers, and Mama was having none of it. She politely squeezed her face as the introductions were made, but it was apparent that she was all the more delighted once they were past the formalities and King Isaac returned to his designated table.

Always one to establish dominance early, Isaac claimed his place at the table and cleared the spaces next to him for his girlfriend and his father. Paul and Irene fell in line with the remaining spots. Isaac asked his timid father if he wanted a beer, and he replied affirmatively, which sent the big man off to retrieve a round for the table.

Bobz was an interesting character. By no means a fatherly figure in the traditional sense, he was a smaller build with a slight hunch to his frame that made Angie nervous because his pack of cigarettes always looked like they were about to fall out of his shirt pocket.

Isaac returned with a beer right as Snacks was coming back around and the younger brother immediately hit him with a guilt trip as to how he, the guest, had to get his dad a beer at his brother's, the resident's, house. This was very much expected by everyone involved as Isaac was not going to forget the fact that he was refused entry to the housing situation while Snacks got the free pass. The older brother replied that he actually bought that beer and just like that the first butting of heads commenced.

That's a shock. Haven't you been unemployed for like a month now? I mean, I was under the impression you had to have a job to live here, King Isaac quipped.

At least I had a job to quit. When's the last time you cashed a check that wasn't from the unemployment office?

Of course, the Saccomanno table was glued to this conversation because they had never seen such intense ribbing. Any outsider would think this was a legit fight, and it kind of was, but for these brothers it was the only way they communicated.

Not that you care, but I'm working at UPS now, Isaac said as he handed his table their drinks. *Georgie got me the interview, and boom, I was in. This is why it's nice to have friends.* He took his seat and began speaking to Paul, signifying that he had tired of Snacks' pathetic excuse for a conversation, so the older brother waved him off and went back into the house.

As the conversations continued, Angie and Jack excused themselves to start firing up the grills and preparing the main course. However, they didn't have much time before they heard a foreign voice say, *Hello*.

They both turned, then immediately abandoned their posts when they saw to their shock and delight that standing right there in the living room was none other than Stanley Norossi. The black sheep of the family had made it. Here he was: the youngest and most distant Norossi.

The front door was open, so I just came in, he said in his gentle manner. He was alone, dressed sharply in his black v-neck and tight charcoal jeans. Right away he demonstrated his nonconformity by handing Angie a bottle of wine, while apologizing for never getting back to her in writing. He spoke much like his father with a very low volume and in short bursts. Angie brought him in for a hug and expressed her joy at finally meeting the man she had heard so much about and she didn't say this, but the man that she had felt a strong connection with from the moment she first opened one of his letters.

He replied how much he had enjoyed getting to know her as of late, and kindly added how Jack had done a poor job of relating her beauty and presence, but then again, even Proust would find trouble doing her features justice. He then did something to Jack she thought she would never see. He went in for a hug and his brother wrapped him around very warmly. Up until that point, she had never seen Jack hug anyone in his family other than his mother, and never had she seen two Norossi brothers come into contact outside of some degree of a physical altercation. The brothers released and Stanley was then led toward the back, with his apprehension already apparent.

Angie had tried to stop for a second to have at least a minute conversation with her pen pal, but the magnetism of the Norossis was too much. The pull of his blood sucked him out the back door and toward his kin. It was so severe, in fact, that Angie worried she would not even get a chance to speak with him at all, adding yet another item to prioritize on her checklist for the day. She only partly realized this, but it was actually this face-to-face that she needed more than anything.

Sure enough, upon sight of their brother, each sibling took their jab.

Oh, shit. Look who found time in his busy Miami schedule to visit the common folk, Isaac began. *How are you going to live in Miami and still come back whiter than all of us?*

Paul continued, *Wait, wait, wait, I got a Herald I keep with me in the car. Do you think you could sign it? It's the one where you gave the oyster place five stars.*

The youngest of the group smiled sheepishly at the attacks and made his way to his father to say hello. His father was very happy to see him, so much that he stood up and gave him a big hug. He then softly told his son that he just won him $20 for a bet he had made with his mother, whom he informed was on her way with Stevey. As Paul and Isaac accordingly began to roast Stevey, Stanley made his way to his pre-determined place at the far seat by Irene, then humbly accepted a Diet Coke from his brother, Jack.

As Angie made her way back to the kitchen to chop up the various burger toppings, she stole a few peeks at her family, reading into every single movement. They were definitely in awe of the Norossis, and she could see all the women licking their chops and taking massive mental notes at what to gossip about once the party concluded. This was the Saccomanno custom: observe and judge. It should have been on their family crest. Even Angie was guilty, although she got the last remaining bit of it, as if there was only enough for two children and she was forced to scrape for whatever was left over. Angie was the only one who could catch herself in the middle of a judgmental stupor, and thus she was the only one who could feel ashamed of it. She had previously made the mistake of catching her mother or sisters in one, only to be rebuked with a shift into the other major Saccomanno trait: denial. She knew that she could never stop their penchant to use any shortcoming in others to prop

103

themselves up, but it was still hard to watch, and especially so in this case when it was the other half of the family she was trying to unite. Her best course of action at this moment was to get the food out quickly and hope everything would settle.

She stopped Jack in the kitchen and firmly asked: *Can you control your brothers?*

What? You know they just play rough.

My mom doesn't know that. They could show like some kind of decorum. Can't you just tell them to cool it?

If I go tell them that, Isaac's just gonna double down. You see how Stanley's dealing, right? He's the master. All he does is smile and let them run out of gas.

Well, tell Snacks to tell him then.

Oh my god, there's literally nothing that would start a fight faster than him doing that.

Forget it! She went back to aggressively cutting onions and tomatoes with a new focus on just letting these people be themselves. She committed wholeheartedly to the delusion that there was nothing wrong with how they were behaving. It was just a different set of values or whatever. It had to be the fear of how her mother was reacting that was making her find them disagreeable when so many times before she had loved their little hangouts. She wasn't going to let the boys' "wild streak" nor her mother's god complex derail this otherwise wonderful afternoon.

Snacks appeared in the kitchen soon after and offered to take control of the grill so Jack and Angie could sit with the family. For Jack, this was more of a punishment than anything, but he figured he could sit with the Saccomannos to smooth things over a bit, so he relinquished his spatula and headed back out.

Angie wasted no time in addressing Snacks. *Hey. I need your help. Can you... keep Isaac in line? You see how he's acting, right?*

Pssh. That guy's nuts, man. If I could do anything, I would. You had to know he'd be extra obnoxious because he still thinks he should be living here.

I know. I know. But if he steps over that line, Jack can't do anything, at least not without you leading, so I need you to... police.

I'll do what I can, Snacks said sheepishly, a side of him she had never seen, and one that she very much wished she was not seeing at a time when she needed his most vicious side to shine. As he made his way out with the raw meat, he added with a quick laugh, *It was your idea to bring us all together.*

Seeing that everything was relatively under control and the guests were enjoying themselves, Angie thought it the perfect time to sit with the Norossis and enjoy their company. She went ahead and pulled up a chair next to Stanley and absorbed the ensuing jabs from everyone at the table speaking of how they've been waiting forever for food and how they expected a higher grade of beer from the fancy Staples Center lady. For her own mental health, she just assumed they were joking and ribbed them right back.

Angie asked Stanley how he was enjoying the party, making sure to add an intonation that conveyed her sarcasm. He intoned right back that it was a blast being back with the family. It was so hard for her not to just immediately jump into a deep conversation with him, but the fact was that the entire subject of that would-be discussion was right there within earshot. As she continued with some stupid small talk about his flight and "How he's been", she peeked over to see if anything would cause this little faction to disperse so she could get into the good gossip. She figured that the food was close to being served and that would spark the table to stand and serve themselves, wherein she could begin a private talk with Stanley. However, in her scheming, she forgot one key element: that the perpetual person of honor had not yet arrived... and no one dared to eat before she did.

Mama Norossi finally emerged not much later, with Stevey following closely behind. As per custom, all the family stood up and gave her hugs as Stevey was immediately grilled about where his wife, daughter and grandkids were, and he had to relay that they couldn't make it, which opened up another session of the boys mocking how little control he had over his own family.

Angie immediately took note of how Bobz shook in his boots as his ex-wife gave him a court kiss on the cheek. Mama Norrossi then gave all her boys a much warmer kiss on both cheeks, even as they tormented the son who drove fifteen miles out of his way to pick her up.

She stopped in disbelief when she saw Stanley, but stood back and waited for him to greet her, while she jabbed at how she hardly recognized him, it had been so long. He gave her a big hug and two kisses on each cheek. As he began to pull back, she yanked him closer and said he owed her a long hug for moving so far away, adding in: *Who knows if I'll ever see you again? I need to cherish every moment.*

After an extended beat, she made it clear the seat next to Stanley was for her. To be fair, she didn't know Angie had already claimed it. Would knowing that have made any difference? Who knows?

For Angie's part, she was far too busy relishing this next moment of presenting her own mother to Jack's and was very pleased to see them meet each other with a long hug as if they had been in-laws for years. They exchanged pleasantries and she made the rounds meeting everyone in the Saccomanno family. Upon the culmination of the formalities, she covertly told Angie that she could tell her family were good people. This warmed her heart deeply until her potential mother-in-law added that it was more than she could say for her lot.

The food had finally been served and the whole situation had calmed a bit in the aftermath of the matriarch's entrance. There was still a bit too much segregation between the families, but Angie began to think that she was expecting far too much. She was trying to force decades of bonds into one afternoon, and that was just not how it worked. Everyone was having a great time. The food was great. The music was perfectly selected. It was a fine event.

Snacks finally made his re-emergence right about then and his mother immediately rose from her seat and waved her hands for him to approach. He obliged and wrapped her in what passed for a hug, leaving just enough room to see the comfort and love through Mama Norossis closed eyelids. Angie was such a sucker for this type of thing that she all but forgot the full year of his transgressions by this sight alone. However, the lovely scene did not last long after the embrace as Mama Norossi quickly began her (playful?) critique of Snacks' employment situation as he took his seat and began eating the chips off Paul's plate.

I'm working on it, ma. It's a tough market right now.

Then how did Isaac get a job? A good one, too. Benefits and everything, right? Now, you won't need to worry about anything when the baby comes, she said to Isaac's shocked girlfriend.

Ma, c'mon, the accused quickly responded, then clarified to the table: *She's not pregnant. Everyone calm down.*

Well, you'd think one of you would give me grandkids. I only get the ones from Stevey, and his wife never lets me see them. I barely even see my own sons, with one living in that hedonistic cesspool under Georgia, and another one attached at the hip to his father.

Bobz did not dare speak up, but had no need as Paul immediately shot down the attack. Stanley refilled Mama Norossis wine glass as he stood up and asked if anyone else needed a drink, to which everyone replied in the affirmative. It was at this moment that Angie sent a quick text to Jack to watch their alcohol intake, which was a top three worry of hers and one that she discussed clearly with Jack repeatedly before the afternoon.

At the Saccomanno table, they had been talking about Charlie's kids and how well they were progressing as hockey players. Oscar loved to brag about his sons, especially to Angie who had the connections to the Los Angeles Kings. Mama Saccomanno naturally loved to hear her grandsons' accomplishments, although she would be quick to excuse herself from a game that could only take place in freezing temperatures.

The discussions continued and it was very much worth a chuckle at how low they spoke compared to how loud the Norossi table was rumbling. Oscar would say something and immediately have to repeat it much louder, until he turned red screaming at his mother-in-law. Angie hoped in vain that this would curb the conversation or at least redirect it since it was heading a little too close to a subject she would rather move past. However, as if enticed by the anxiety itself, all the talk of these glorious grandchildren went ahead and once again made its way toward how she herself had none.

I'm sure we'll see a baby bump any day now, Bee said.

Charlie added, *And they'll be so beautiful. You guys have that look. Jack has those boyish features and if they get your hair, my god.*

Angie went along with it and even let it slip that she really does feel they'll marry within a year or so. It could have been her own doubts projecting, but it appeared as if no one expressed much excitement at the estimate. She was not sure how to take these muted reactions. Maybe they just didn't believe her, which was bad enough, but she even went as far as to think that they weren't exactly thrilled at the idea of spending more time with those crazy Sicilians across the patio. It was glaringly obvious now that these two came from very different stock and the adaptations would take time, but it couldn't be that bad... right? What a complete disaster if the Saccomannos left today with that as the takeaway. It was such a painful thought that she shoved it right back down and changed the subject.

Despite Angie's warning--and in hindsight, how completely idiotic of her to think Jack had any ability whatsoever to control his family--the Norossis were getting noticably drunker as the night went on. She had been a part of their high-octane partying before, but obviously she would just be a spectator today. She had even flirted with the idea of not having any alcohol available, but her naivete shone brightly as she scrapped the idea and put all her chips on the boys being responsible and mature by themselves.

Mama Norossi remarked to her family at how beautiful Bee and Charlie's children were, and how much they resembled their lovely grandmother, but then immediately spun it into a guilt trip against every son, and somehow, even Bobz.

Jack is my best hope, except he looks like his father, so even if his genes beat Angela's, I'm sure it'll just be a little Bobz. He'll be a handsome boy, but not as striking as he would be if he looked like me. Look at Stanley. He's my spitting image. What a beautiful man. He just has the wandering eye of his father, so I'll never see him settle down. He's too busy breaking the hearts of every Cuban on that peninsula.

Mom--, Stanley tried to interject under a blush that struck Angie as more ashamed than embarrassed. Her initial feeling was that his promiscuity was so bad that his own mother knew it, but that didn't seem to make sense. She then figured it had to do with how he wanted to settle down too, but he was finding no luck, similar to how she struggled with setting a plan to marry and bear children with Jack. This somehow didn't make total sense to her either, but she hit an impasse as to why that was. She made a mental note to look out for that tint of red to see if it appeared from any other trigger.

Mama Norossi continued: *No, no. The girls were always flooding you and now you're richer and even more cultured, and it all does me no good. The saddest part is that you'll probably still be the next one to marry, and then you'll have kids but you'd just raise them in South Beach, anyway. I'll just have to keep praying that these ones work fast. They like to act like I'll live forever. Maybe I should have re-married, if only for the chance to have step-children like Beatrice and Charlotte, who bear such beautiful children and without waiting until their mother is old to do it.*

Paul tried to relax his mother, but Isaac jumped in and told him that he shouldn't say anything since he had the longest tenured relationship of any of them, and he and Irene aren't even engaged. Snacks jumped in and accused Isaac of speaking out of turn since he'd be the last one to have a kid since his girlfriends don't even make it

109

through one menstrual cycle with him. This set off a huge argument which was the only course of action with Snacks having crossed that line right in front of Becky, who grew very heated especially because she was only about ten days or so away from her own cycle beginning again, and despite the invitation to this huge family ordeal, she had felt that Isaac had been recently growing cold toward her. She began defending herself and soon enough the entire table was arguing (except of course Bobz) and the dynamics of the Norossi family were on full display for all in attendance.

King Isaac raised his voice as high as he could and Snacks spoke even more snarky to him in response. Stevey so very foolishly made his appeals to reason and Paul tried to interject, but rarely made any headway. A powerless Jack shook his head in shame as he looked over to Stanley, who was completely unphased as someone should be when every single family gathering devolved into shouting matches just like this. He simply comforted his mother as she continued her own complaints.

Meanwhile, the Saccomannos stopped all conversation and tried their best to follow the Norossis' developments. The men were simply spectating as they would any televised bout and the women were no doubt absorbing the most details they could to their memory so they could talk about this moment for realistically the rest of their lives. Angie, however, was in the midst of a much more introspective, and painful, process.

This was a key moment in her relationship with Jack, as she had been telling herself for weeks before she even announced a plan to host. Of course, she didn't plan for it to head in this particular direction, but she had now accepted it and moved past that foolish hope. What she now focused on was that this was her new family. She didn't even know at this point that this was how they always behaved, yet Snacks' words were ringing wiser and wiser as she saw the detonation take place not ten feet from her as a result of bringing this family together. These people with whom she would soon (she still hoped) spend every single major holiday were overgrown children in terms of maturity and emotional control. Perhaps worst of all was the undeniable fact that her husband was powerless against them. Would this impotence augment as he aged? Had she already ignored the red flag Norossi traits that she judged so harshly in his brothers? These ponderings flooded her head as Isaac stood up and got in Stevey's face, triggering the other brothers to stand as well to try to diffuse the situation that had grown far too intense.

In pure instinct, she sought out Snacks to help, knowing clearly that Jack would have no success, but in the confusion, she hadn't seen that once again, he had disappeared.

Isaac and Stevey were now bumping and pushing each other, and the former was more and more violently pushing off Paul as he tried to pull him back, knocking bottles of beer and chip bowls onto the floor. Mama Norossi had officially washed her hands of the situation, yelling out that she had had enough and this was yet another regretful event. Stanley escorted her inside, crushing any hope of Angie's much-anticipated one-on-one with him and also, leaving Bobz stranded out here in the belly of the beast.

The shouting continued, as did the fits of pushing, until Isaac slapped Stevey a little too hard and the older brother shoved his hand into Isaac's face. Paul sheepishly tried to pull Stevey back, but he only ended up getting caught up in the shove as Isaac dropped his pad level and pushed the two all the way backward into the pool, just barely missing Bee's little girl in the process.

Both tables stood up and rushed to the scene as the boys continued to wrestle in the water until their low level of cardiorespiratory fitness finally brought the battle to an end. Jack quickly emerged with towels for the three participants and the boys sat on opposite ends of the backyard drying off.

Angie went to her sisters to make sure the kids were okay. She tried her hardest to avoid eye contact altogether, but a quick glance into Bee's irises sent her stomach into knots. She was too embarrassed to even apologize and instead retreated into the kitchen to fix some to-go plates as everyone gathered their things.

When he was mostly dried off, Isaac stood up violently and said firmly (and within ear shot of several guests under the age of ten): *Fuck this shit. I'm sorry, Jacky, I'm out, and I'm not fucking coming back to anything where that piece of shit's gonna be here. Him or Snacks!*

Everyone stood by in silence as Isaac stormed out with Becky following. From that point, everyone else took that cue to take their exits as well. Unfortunately for Angie, she would be subject to everyone rushing their thanks to her in the kitchen on their way out, making it that much harder for her to suppress the imminent breakdown she was defending against. In an odd way, it actually eased her when some guests were even compelled to say that they were looking forward to the next event. In almost any other circumstance, it would have caused her to bust out laughing.

Bee, Charlie, and Mama were the last to leave. They offered to help clean up a little, but Angie was firm in denying them. All were careful to not mention the fight or anything else that happened previous to it, but instead kept it short and lied about how they enjoyed the party. She could see the disappointment in Mama's eyes and… it hurt really badly. This was the polar opposite of what she was seeking and she was nowhere near prepared for those soft hazel eyes' simultaneous transmission of concern and judgment. It took everything she had left to keep from breaking down into tears right then and there, but she somehow managed to hold it all in. With one last hug, she bid her tribe goodbye.

Jack was smart enough to avoid any debriefing right away and instead just focused on cleaning up the back. Angie worked on the kitchen, washing the serving utensils as she considered where exactly she went wrong. The course of the evening was clearly her responsibility and she wouldn't do herself the disservice of just pointing the finger at Isaac, Snacks, Jackson, or anyone else. Was it really that wrong to invite the whole family like that? Surely, the answer was not to always keep the

112

guest list tiered so that the Triumvirate never ran into the Bottom Feeders and the old war had no choice but to rekindle. Was her life really going to be an eternal social chemistry experiment?

Try as she might, she couldn't shake what she finally concluded was a form of betrayal by the night's co-host. She really expected more of her boyfriend, especially when she was pretty much analyzing his every action to see how her eventual husband and father of her children would rise during times of duress. This had not been the best audition. He was obviously at the bottom of the totem pole when it came to family dynamics, but this was his home. A man should defend his home. She knew this was what her mother was thinking the entire time, and she agreed with her. If these were his own brothers, how would he handle a home invasion or any kind of outside threat from a stranger? This was itself jumping the gun--but maybe it was related after all--because he hadn't even spoken about marriage, much less proposed. Even if her mother had arrived with the seed of disappointment in how they were not married, she might have left with the bud of fear that they would actually get married.

Then there was Snacks. For a moment there, he almost had her fooled. He did such a fantastic job preparing the party, then was unable to de-escalate a fight, then was nowhere to be found when it boiled over. What an idiot to actually trust this man. Had she completely forgotten the past year? Yet through all of this dissection, she was still careful not to pluck that low-hanging fruit.

This was her fault for not seeing the bigger picture. She had put too much faith into factors that needed her leadership. Where she had cut corners was where the strings began to unravel and there was no hiding from it. Of course, she was not the only person who needed improvement and if this were a work project under her direction, she would hit several persons with some acute criticisms, but that would come later. For now, she needed to clean her house. Once again, she'd have to do it without the help of her tenant, but at least the man who mattered was here. She would simply lick her wounds and maybe even try again at some point.

It was crucial that above all--in spite of everything that had been botched this evening, and all the cumulative errors she had committed during this failure--she simply needed to move forward.

THE BABY

Angie often had down time at the office, especially on the days when she had later hours to accommodate an event at Staples Center. This happened more often during the colder months since the arena hosted the Kings as well as two NBA teams.

She had grown even more pensive since the Memorial Day Debacle and it was at these times that her mind really wandered. She thought about the stereotype that every woman begins planning her wedding as a little girl, and how they create a Prince Charming in their minds. Then when they meet a man, they can project this creation onto him to varying degrees and that can lead them into abusive relationships or ones with terminal power imbalances. She wondered if there were women who were able to skip this step. She had thought she was one of them, but now all she ever thought about was how she was unmarried and without child. This never concerned her before, but after living with her boyfriend for over a year, the thought was inescapable.

There was also the laundry list of other issues when it came to bearing and raising children. What about her career? She could get the maternity leave, but that wouldn't solve the considerable political implications of missing that much time. She was rising so fast in the company and if her career took precedence, it was far too early to have a child. Then again, in the perpetual realm of corporate ladder climbing, when would the time ever be "right"? As all these factors swarmed her headspace, she couldn't help but wonder at the irony of how someone with such security in her life could feel so lost.

That evening, Angie met Jack at a restaurant in Koreatown after work. She always liked this place because it was so loud and busy inside. Much like Staples Center, she found comfort in the chaos, that is as long as it didn't have to directly involve her. They both ordered the big combo meal with the soup, rice, and all the goodies, and sat patiently waiting.

It had been a week with its own unique ups and downs, and the general demands from her supervisors had whittled her down to the bone by the time Friday came around. The time had also just changed so both were getting a hit of that seasonal depression that came with the earlier nights. She looked across the table at her partner as his beady eyes scanned the crowd around them. He looked ready to crash and it was adorable. She did her best to mask a huge grin as the eyes made their way to hers and he tried to spark up some typical dinner conversation. Quickly and decisively, she rerouted the conversation to more significant subject matter.

You want kids, right? The words came out so fast they confused Jack. It was as if he had to decode them and understand exactly what she had just asked because the sentence itself was just so big to lead with like that. He replied, *Sure,* in the most nonchalant way that was exactly the opposite tone his girlfriend needed to hear at that moment.

You know I'm not 'that' kind of girlfriend, but I've just been thinking about how great it's been living together. It doesn't even feel like a year. She paused with this because even saying it out loud was still foreign. *We're slowly approaching being together for a decade. It's so crazy.*

She wanted to pause here, but instead just powered right through to: *I don't even care about a ceremony, or a ring, or whatever. I think… what it comes down to honestly, is fear. I never thought I was an insecure person, but I can't imagine what I'd do without you. You know… I love you. Look, I'm not trying to pressure you, okay? I don't need anything from you. I just want to like let you know where my head's been at.*

Jack was naturally taken aback by this brash honesty, but he replied coolly that he enjoyed the past year together too and felt the same way about it being incomprehensible to imagine being with anyone else but her. Angie was honest with herself and admitted that this was not good enough, but she was also wise enough to realize that she couldn't expect him to pop the question right now, so she eased a bit.

Do you want kids? I know you say you do, but like is that in your five year plan?

Yeah. I've always wanted kids. I just figure that you have to coordinate with your job, which I know is important to you, so I'd probably just take your cue on it.

What if I said I wanted them now?

Angie surprised herself with the wielding of this test. Her sisters used to do this to her when they were growing up. For example, if they had been spending the day playing doll house, Bee might ask her if she could use one of her doll's dresses to make an accessory for her own doll, knowing that it was Angie's favorite. After Angie thought about it, tried to suggest an alternative, and finally relented, peeling the dress off the toy and handing it over, Bee would say she changed her mind, having been satisfied with merely the potential of the sacrifice.

Now that she was thinking more about it, her mother still did this. She had called recently to set up a brunch date with her and after discussing a new place they wanted to try, Mama expressed a concern that it would be out of her price range. Angie assured her that it would be fine and that she would treat her regardless, as her own special honor. Of course, when the check came after the meal, Mama insisted on paying her half. It was only in this very moment, that Angie suspected that it might have been more of a test than a change of heart.

Jack looked at Angie and right away said that he would be okay with that. They needed to plan a little more, of course, but there's no reason he could think that they shouldn't have kids right now, if she wanted that. These were only words and they only carried so much weight, but they still put Angie at ease. Many men wouldn't even agree via verbal contract when presented with such a hasty proposal, but Jack did.

They continued their meal speaking of less life-changing subjects. Angie had received all the reassurance she needed for the time being, but she still missed the unsaid. Just as sex was easier to get that love, or any form of commitment, a child was easier to get than marriage. She secured a verbal contract that children were on the horizon, but what she really should have focused on was a contract to validate their partnership and tie it in some sort of ceremony. That's what she really wanted after all. This was a solid step in the right direction, but when one attacks, one must attack at the foundation.

This would end up being the exact situation that would teach Angie this valuable lesson.

...

With so much happening so fast, Snacks was able to coast by another couple months without paying any rent and Angie had not even noticed. He had been smart enough to tone down some of his more annoying habits and kept his part of the house clean-ish, so she had no reason to pester him. The same indifference that Snacks had cultivated in his mother, then his roommates, was in full force as Angie began sweeping his crumbs off the counter and washing his dishes without even noticing that she was cleaning up after him. Of course, she was always cleaning up after Jack in most cases, so it would have been difficult for her to discern anyway.

What disrupted this balance was actually Jack being unable to keep a secret. He let it slip in conversation that Snacks had been seeing someone. Naturally, Angie showed no restraint in asking follow-up questions about the development. She wasn't so much curious as she was shocked. Snacks hadn't had a girlfriend or even a date to her knowledge since he lived with them and she never thought he would, especially not in the midst of unemployment.

She learned that the mystery woman's name was Jessica, and she was actually an old acquaintance of his from High School. She was now divorced and the two had re-connected at a local watering hole. They kept seeing each other at the bar and eventually started meeting up outside of the establishment. This had been going on for about two months or so and the only reason Jack knew was that one of their mutual friends had seen them out and about and wasted no time in informing Jack about the sight.

Angie wanted to know more about this girl, but Jack barely knew her at all. The only thing he was able to relay was that he remembered that Snacks made a remark back when he was in high school. For whatever reason, he confided in Jack that he thought she was cute for a redhead. This revelation had come unprovoked and unexpected, and oddly enough, it had been the only time Jack could remember him ever talking to him about girls.

Snacks was not a ladies man, per se, but he never lacked from the attention of the opposite sex. Despite his off-putting habits and sometimes very noticeable odor, he still had that priceless charm. He used the same tactics to impress women that he did to manipulate literally everyone around him, and thus, his success rate was higher than the average. Now, he was never going to be seen out with a true stunner, but his dates were pretty and they were always out of his league as far as looks and economic status.

It had really been interesting that he hadn't dated since he moved in with Angie and Jack, but that was only what Angie had noticed. For all she knew, he had a girl in his bed with him every night, using their shower and eating their food. He was that sneaky.

Angie saw no problem with him dating, other than the obvious. Dating meant that money was being spent. She was sure that he was mooching off Jessica excessively and foolishly hoped that he wasn't taking too much advantage of her. The fact that he had been seeing her regularly eased her thoughts, but not by much.

The other issue tied to the first. Since he was unemployed, he didn't really need another distraction. Hanging out with his girlfriend would be taking time away from his job search and thus taking cash out of hers and Jack's pocket.

She was already dreading the thought of having to check in on his job search, making sure that he was actually trying to find work instead of just enjoying the time off. It was only natural to slack when you had a guaranteed roof over your head, so she didn't judge him for lagging, but it was in her best interest to keep him on task, or else she would have to do the even harder task of kicking him out.

Even though she prayed it would never come to that, from their recent discussions about marriage and children, Angie felt much better about that ultimate option. Jack was very much in love with her and perhaps for the first time ever, she felt confident that he would choose a life with her over a continued residence with his brother, if he absolutely had to.

Knowing this, she could worry a little less and focus all of her spare energy on the task of finally getting her tenant to pay up.

A big theory that started floating around at this time was if Snacks had locked down a girlfriend because his mother's talk about not having enough grandchildren embarrassed him. Surely, as the oldest boy, he had committed the biggest failure in this regard since he had sired none.

Angie was always worried that she was underestimating Snacks. She knew he used that natural inclination to his advantage very often and she never wanted to fall for such an elementary snare. She was exponentially more intelligent than him, but he had his advantages and he never shied away from using them. Could someone as self-centered and seemingly unbothered be affected like this? Or was she drawing too simple a conclusion from the unrelated and meaningless fact that the dude was getting laid regularly now?

That was the other thing. She hoped… like really hoped, they weren't having sex in her house. It pissed her off that he even had her thinking that this man has and will continue to have sex. There have been women who have engaged in such an intimate, close act with Snacks Norossi--that was a thought upon which she NEVER wanted to reflect.

This then led to the reality of this situation, which was Snacks acting in a way that could potentially create a little Snacks. She had spent a great deal of time thinking about what kind of father Jack would be.

She used tiny moments and actions he took to build a picture, and she was not always happy with the final product, if she was being honest. However, Snacks was very much still a child himself. She couldn't imagine him and Jessica making one bad decision and bringing a child into the world under their parentage. This was not just unfair to the child, but it was unfair to Snacks, who would then have to break his rituals of frozen TV dinners and all-night Adam Sandler movie marathons to change diapers and push strollers. Even if there was any chance that he was now interested in being a dad, he was clearly not ready for the role.

Angie worried that Jessica was not aware of this. The fact that she was willingly spending time with Snacks in a romantic way meant this was not a woman who saw things clearly. He might even be singing her sweet songs of anything she wants to hear, which to a divorcée would work wonders, depending on how long she had been single or how many failed relationships had followed her broken marriage. Add to the fact that she was a woman over forty who had never had kids, and she was dead to rights under that man.

Snacks was definitely smart enough to realize a big fish when he caught one and Jessica could very well be his ticket out of here. This certainly made more sense than him wanting a child. Angie was sure he would give Jessica a dozen children if it meant he could live with her and be supported. She was unsure of how rich Jessica was, but she assumed it was enough to entice Snacks to dig into his toolbox to at least find out.

Then again, maybe Snacks was in love. He had to be so lonely in his situation. It seemed like he had a decent crush on Jessica back in high school and maybe now fate stepped in to give him what he needs right now. Maybe this is what they both need. Or perhaps it's a combination of everything. Maybe Snacks and Jessica are in love. They found a way to avoid the crushing loneliness of single late adulthood. She has a path to having a child. He has a new financial support system. And of course, Angie would have a way to rid herself of the leech. Why should she worry herself when everything was working out so well?

...

Angie was more scared than surprised to find a letter from Stanley waiting for her on the table when she got home from work. She felt that she had greatly embarrassed herself in front of him and was definitely not going to write to him again after that fiasco. She assumed she would never be contacted by him and was taking solace in this time between having to interact with him again. By this point, being spared the shame had outweighed the disappointment of losing her new friend. Yet, here he was, resuming their correspondence.

She held it for a moment to feel how many pages were included the way she used to check for college acceptance letters. This time she was more unsure though, because a thick envelope could be a detailed criticism. He was a professional writer after all, and would have no trouble attacking her with every possible barb of the English language. On the other hand, a thin envelope could be as simple as him asking her to never write to him again. The fact remained that this letter was rather thick.

Finally, she managed to just brush off all the speculation and appreciate the fact that he took the time to write, at least once more.

Dear Angie,

I'm very sorry I had to leave your party so quickly and under those circumstances. I'm sure you understand I didn't want to cause any more confusion, and I figured that you would want to decompress without the added pressure of seeing me off.

It really was a beautiful party in a gorgeous home and I was happy to have been a part. It goes without saying I hope, but if you are ever in the Miami area, please let me know and you are more than welcome to stay with me or give me an opportunity to show you some of the city's best spots.

Now, I don't really know how to start this part. I'll admit I was worried about writing to you like this. I thought a lot about just calling you and then I ended up writing a few drafts of this letter... if I'm being honest, it came down to the fact that I can tell that you are a good person. I like to think I'm good at reading that in people. Don't get too charmed, because if you weren't so pure, I wouldn't be telling you this next part, which you may not want to hear.

As odd as it may sound, I'm glad that you were able to see my family like that because I can assure you that virtually every party I have ever attended with them has ended just like yours did. Maybe you know this from Jack. I admit part of me wanted to tell you this when you invited me, but for some reason (maybe because it was a new house?) I thought this time might be different. That's probably why I worked it out so that I could attend.

I'm sure you've guessed by now that I live away from my family for a reason. I'm not going to go into detail for time's sake and because it's still a family (and thus, private) affair, but again, I'm positive you've ascertained the basics already.

Unfortunately, you have "Snacks" as a tenant in your home--something I wouldn't wish on my worst enemy. I can only imagine what that's truly been like, but feel free to vent to me anytime you like. Just know this: he is a <u>liar</u> and more than likely a <u>narcissist</u>. It's not all his fault, but **<u>trust nothing he tells you</u>**.

There's something else. Please forgive me in advance for being so direct, but trust I'm telling you this because I want you to have full disclosure since you and my

125

brother have been together for a good amount of time now and of course, own property together, which makes me assume marriage and children are on the horizon.

All of this will continue.

It will continue for your entire life if you choose to make yours concurrent with Jackson's.

I won't pretend to know your relationship with my brother, but please understand the cost. I saw your reaction at the barbeque and I empathized greatly. Imagine growing up in an environment like that, except it was you who was always the easiest target. Our family was problematic in its own way as all families are, but the personalities ours birthed are... the nice way to put it would be: unique.

Again, I'm sure you've seen it, so I won't waste your time in writing it down here.

Forgive me for saying this, but Jackson is not exempt from this... for lack of a better word: genetic curse. I'm not either. I'll tell you that I've been very proactive about my therapy for almost a decade now and I firmly believe I need consistent professional help to undo a lot of the problems inherent with my genes and my upbringing. I've recommended seeing a doctor to Jackson many times--he's the only one I would even bring that up to--with almost no luck. (Maybe it's something you'd consider discussing with him?)

I don't want to ramble. I just want to do you the courtesy of telling you what I've experienced and letting you make your future choices off the information. Take it how you will.

I would love to have you in our family. I love that you make my brother so happy. He's always telling me how much he adores you. I just want you to make sure you're happy for yourself and not for any other potentially synthetic reason.

Please feel more than free to reply to me about this or any subject. Or just call.

I'll be looking forward to it.

With love,
Stanley

...

The following week, Angie received some more good news at her work. She had been talking with one of the executives with whom she had developed a strong networking relationship and he was able to give her contact information for a supervisor in the maintenance department at a small venue in east L.A. Angie was thrilled because she used to book events for that particular venue so she would easily be able to strike up a conversation with this person and hopefully get Snacks a job setting up and maintaining the sound system.

Her big mistake was not telling Snacks about this first.

She made the call to the supervisor and explained how she got his info, how she used to book shows there, and then went right into the job opportunity. The supervisor was happy to take her recommendation with great weight and was absolutely thrilled to get such a well-connected applicant in the mix. He told her to just give him the contact info for Snacks' former supervisor and if it all checked out, he'd bring him in for an interview and they would go from there. She was so determined to get this ball rolling, all she had to do was shuffle a few papers to find the phone number and she gave it to him right then and there. With a few more words of praise for Snacks that almost set her tongue on fire, she said goodbye and went back to work.

A few weeks had gone by without her having heard back from the supervisor. She was reluctant to ask Snacks about it, because she knew he would be upset that she had stepped in, but she didn't think he would be so upset that he would reject the job offer. The next time she saw him around the house, she gently asked him about the job search and he didn't mention being contacted by anyone. All he did was launch into a fifteen minute tirade of how he's been pounding the pavement, but no one wants skilled labor anymore, the economy is in the toilet, and an array of other lies/excuses. As impatient as ever, she called her contact once again, just to check in for him.

That's when she found out the truth.

Snacks didn't quit his job in a heroic display of solidarity with his staff. He had been fired for stealing. From what she understood, he had first not shown up for a shift. After trying to contact him over and over, the manager called in a replacement. This fill-in went about the normal duties for that position and during an inventory check, he found a huge discrepancy with the stock of various connectors and a few speakers. Of course, these were in a place to which only the managers and Snacks had the key. Angie had to immediately flood her contact with apologies on Snacks' behalf and on her own. She had not only burned her reputation with this contact by recommending the thief, but she had also threatened the relationship between him and the executive through which they had connected. This was the biggest issue of the moment. Snacks would be dealt with later, but burning this extremely important political dynamic within the Los Angeles live entertainment industry would need to be mended post haste or her career might never recover.

This time around, she didn't tell Jack anything. She was so angry with this latest mishap, she wanted Snacks all to herself. No one was going to soften her approach or talk her out of ripping into this overgrown child. To be honest, this was the best thing she could do for him. He had literally found a way to steal from his workplace, embarrass his landlord, and pay no consequences for any of it. In fact, he had managed to gain from it. He now lived comfortably rent-free, had a lot more time to watch Netflix and war documentaries, and now he had a steady girlfriend that he was grooming for his next big move.

Angie had had enough of all of it. Snacks had only been an annoyance until now: a few boxes left out, dirty dishes, fingerprints all over the microwave, etc. She even felt guilty often enough of how much she complained about his quirks, but now, he was committing crimes and putting her and Jack in danger of being involved as accomplices. Most of all, he was now putting her career at risk. He could be a mooch all he wanted. He could spend his time goofing off and satisfying his basest of pleasures, but he would not do it at the expense of her and he was not going to continue doing this in her home. His time was up and she was going to end it tonight.

Angie had intended on confronting Snacks that very night, but her rage was so extreme she was honestly afraid she would kill him. The horrible truth was that no matter what, she would have to do her best not to let her anger push her to say things that could not be taken back. She was not just kicking out some lowlife tenant. This was going to be her brother-in-law at some point very soon, and she didn't want to drive that wedge between Jack and Snacks, and by doing so, become the villain of the family. She had to be firm, but tactful.

Right now was not the time to act, so instead of improvising the talk with him then and there, she headed to bed, took a couple sleeping pills, and knocked out into a state where there were no tenants, no brothers-in-law, and no Norossis.

She chose to work from home the next day and got up early to prepare for the moment ahead. Angie was so serious, she brewed her coffee and sat at her desk with a notepad, immediately brainstorming points and putting them in an order so she could be as efficient as possible when she laid into her tenant. Part of her was deeply disturbed that she had to go through this effort when it was her house and she should be able to remove a tenant if they wore shoes she didn't like. Yet, she knew that this wasn't how it worked and unfortunately, she would need to communicate better if she wanted this to go as smoothly as possible.

After a bit of work, she had a plan. It was only 08:30 by this point, so she knew she could work for another few hours until he woke up. Having an excess of time like this wasn't really a positive because all the rage from last night had now deformed into anxiety. She was incredibly scared of confronting her boyfriend's brother and now she almost wished she had told Jack so they could've put up a united front. The thought of giving him his notice to vacate without having cleared it with Jack was starting to sound more and more shady. Plus, Snacks would most definitely bring up the integral point that the man paying half the mortgage would need to okay it, and she would have to give her boldness some gas and tell him that he need not worry about that because she had already decided it is either him moving or her, and he was welcome to wait and see who Jack chose. Yes, this was going to be messy any way she went about it.

Snacks emerged from his room just after 13:00 and Angie was right there at the kitchen table, waiting for him. He did his thing where he walked past her with no eye contact or even a head turn and said a quick, *Mornin',* and Angie replied back with a full, enunciated, *Good Morning.* He opened the fridge, drank his jug of water for a few long seconds and then closed it back up. That's when Angie began.

Snacks, are you doing anything right now?

I was going to go to the store and get some waffles or something, but no big plans, why?

Angie paused for the slightest moment while she weighed the impact of her next tactic, taking the time to just... have a good look at him. He slept in literally the same clothes he would wear that day: an AC/DC t-shirt and cargo shorts. He even still had yesterday's white crew socks on. She made eye contact with him and saw nothing behind the faded blue irises. She was trying to send a telepathic message of how she knew about at least this lie, but he wouldn't flinch. This last hope of maybe avoiding the confrontation by having him fold and admit it

130

himself was destined to fail. Like every major problem in her life, she would have to solve it herself.

I know what happened at Best Buy.

He quickly shot out, *Yeah, those fu--*

Stop. Upon this command, he tilted his head in confusion which made Angie think that no one had ever told him to stop talking before and he was unsure what to do when instructed. She herself was surprised he actually obeyed her command. *I know you were fired. Don't say anything. Do you want to sit for a second?*

May I speak?

Just sit down and listen to what I have to say. Can you do that please?

Always the strategist, Snacks knew the best option was to sit and stay quiet until he knew her exact intent with this meeting. He took a seat, folded his arms, and prepared for battle.

Angie told him about the recommendation she had given him and how it had come back to her. He remained silent as she qualified her information with the disclaimer that she wanted to hear from him what happened and why exactly he did it and then lied about it.

Once given permission he launched into: *People take connectors and stupid shit like that all the time. When people return things, we sell them back at a lower price and sometimes the customer says they don't need connectors, so we just put them in a box. I've let guys take a chord or two, whatever, because they just sit there. We can't even put them in the system, because they have no inventory ID or barcode. They just used this as an excuse to get me out because I was already raising hell about the cut hours!*

Well, what about the speakers?

I bought those. I bought the four big ones and grabbed a broken one that was sitting there. Again, it had no number on it and it literally couldn't be sold. I took it home, re-wired some of it, got it working again, and installed it. That store lost nothing from me taking that speaker. I'm telling you they wouldn't give one shit if anyone else did that, but for me they made an example to keep everyone else from complaining about the bullshit they were pulling.

If all that's true, why did you lie about it?

Because look how you're reacting, I knew you wouldn't believe the real story.

Angie had been expecting a challenging match-up because Snacks was clearly the strongest manipulator she had ever met, but she was still impressed by how quickly he could lie and construct an airtight story. Even if he had sat down and worked out a perfect alibi, it was worthy of praise at how he had seen every single objection coming and had an out-route for each one of them. She continued with a newfound gameplan.

How did you get them to not prosecute you?

It wasn't stealing! They had no case. Legally, they couldn't do anything and really I should've countersued for wrongful termination. Add that to the dozen other things they've done to me.

If we're going to talk about this, you have to stop lying. Stop exaggerating and twisting facts, and just tell me the truth. No matter what happened, you don't have a job, you aren't getting any unemployment, and now you're living with us and using our stuff for free. I'm telling you, you're going to have to leave, like very soon.

Jesus! I've been busting my ass for weeks trying to get a job. Give me a break! And when I'm not looking for work, I'm spending hour after hour every day fixing all the shit around here!

You're going to have a hard time finding any work if your supervisor is telling these guys you stole from them. Do you not see that? You've only had that one job pretty much your whole life. How is anyone going to trust you now? Do you really not realize how screwed you are?

Yeah, I've been screwed my whole life. Couldn't even piss right from the moment I came out of the womb. Always getting the short straw and never getting any help from anyone. I'm fucking used to it.

Snacks, we've been sheltering you for more than a year. I've welcomed you into our home. You've used the water, the internet, the

132

food--all those things Jack and I paid for and you never made any attempt to pay us even just a base rent.

I tried!

I'm not talking about that. I'm talking about the months before-- She stopped herself here, readjusting to her plan of not getting sucked into his red herrings and other traps. *You know I vouched for you. Like put my reputation on the line. Who knows how many clients and contacts I've burned because of your lying. Do you understand that?*

I never asked you to do that. You should've just stood out of it.

I can't stay out of it, Snacks. You're leeching off me constantly. I need to do something to get you off the couch because you're so lost, or whatever it is, that you don't even see the hole you've dug yourself into.

Snacks shook his head in frustration. This very well could have been the first time he had ever been backed into a corner. He really hadn't thought far enough to realize that not only did he only have one reference, but it was a massively negative one. Of course, he had no education or any real skills. His only hope was finding a friend who could hire him, but he didn't have many anymore and none of those few were much better off than him. He had to admit to himself that he had no idea how he would continue now and in fact, that thought scared him tremendously. Now, his only shelter was about to evaporate and it wasn't a flimsy Norossi he had to conquer to save himself. Angela Saccomanno was tough. She wasn't going to be broken easily. All of this flooded him at once and he started to crack.

So what, I have a couple weeks to leave? Then I'm on the street?

Stop it. You're not going on the street. Look, I asked you to be honest, so I'll be honest, too. I wanted you out of here like six months ago. I'm sure you could tell. If you had found a job right away and started paying your fair share, maybe we wouldn't be talking like this right now and if you were a... nicer person and maybe a more helpful tenant, we possibly wouldn't be here, but the fact is, you'd have to leave at some point. When we have kids and this becomes our family home, are you just going to hang out in your room? Like, you see how that's weird, right?

Snacks knew the writing on the wall very well, of course, but he would never give Angie the satisfaction of seeing her words qualified by his approval. He thought about snapping back that he had already secured his escape route, but he wasn't ready to pull that string just yet.

True, his relationship with Jessica had ulterior motives, but he did in fact like her and he was enjoying the time spent together for more reasons than the fact that she was paying for everything. She had already expressed how much she liked Snacks and how he was so authentic and unfiltered, blah blah blah. The point being clearly that she was falling in love with him and seeing him more and more seriously as a long term partner as time went on. Snacks was elated by this fact because he knew his time with Angie would run out and at a much faster rate now that he was jobless. The timing was impeccable and the best part was he would not have to work. He could be a stay-at-home husband (maybe father, too), have an attractive partner, and be set for life. The only issue was that he could under no circumstances rush this crucial step. If he forced her hand and asked to move in, she might become suspicious. (He had never asked for anything from her. She always offered.) If she found out he had no other alternative, she might start to see him as a bum and would immediately pull her own escape chord in response. Snacks needed a little more time.

I know, I know, he said. *Shit. That job was my life. I know that sounds stupid because it's fucking Best Buy, but I've been there for a decade plus. I had reputation and respect there. And you're right, who would hire me now? I didn't even do anything, but it's like how you're saying, no one will believe me. I'm just a thief now. I mean, I'm asking around for work. I can still work. I'm a good worker. I got leadership experience. It's just… I'm going crazy trying to get back out there. It's hard! It's never been this hard.*

I understand. I do. I wish I could help. I'm sure Jack does, too. The only thing I would do is tell you to use me as a personal reference, but I can't honestly recommend you for anything.

I know, I wouldn't want you to. He dropped his head and began aggressively rubbing his forehead. *Shit! I'm sorry. I should've come clean from the start. If you lost your job because of me, I would've felt like shit. Honestly, I never thought you'd do something like that for me.*

Just because you get on my nerves doesn't mean I don't see you as family. You have to understand that distinction. If I'm asking you to leave, it's because that's the landlord-tenant part of our relationship. We never should've started that part to be honest. I was worried about how you would make it without us, but now I'm even more worried. At least you had an income back then.

Snacks thanked her again and once more expressed his understanding. He went on to another long spiel that Angie politely sat through, but maintained that he had four weeks to find a job and pay them the $500 or he would have to vacate. He determined that his best course of action in that moment would be to agree. He could use more aggressive tactics as the date grew closer, but the present demanded civility. He shifted gears into:

Okay. That's fair. I mean… I don't have a right to oppose. I know that. Four weeks. Okay. I'll try my best. Get what I can in order. That's all I can do, right?

It is, she said firmly. She softened for a beat to advise him to also create a contingency plan. She reaffirmed that she was available to him in any realistic way, but as is always the case, the world is not a bowling lane with bumpers on it, sometimes one rolls a gutter ball on a crucial attempt.

Having come to an understanding, she released him back to his room, where she liked to think he immediately logged into Indeed to check for openings, but deep down, she knew he was just going to fire up Netflix and watch another episode of some sitcom from the 90's. The difference now was that the deal was made and it was his clock that was running. She had truly done all she could. The rest was now completely up to him, and she didn't care particularly which route he chose.

A few nights later, Angie arrived home and began thumbing through the day's mail that Snacks had retrieved. She had spoken with Jack about their ultimatum the night before and her hot streak continued as she once again got him to agree to the stipulation verbally, although (once again) she was a bit unsure how this would unfold in practice. She hadn't had to give him the me-or-him ultimatum quite yet, so she still had that bullet loaded, but she knew that using it would incur collateral damage that could scar their relationship permanently.

There were so many obstacles to navigate in any relationship and she realized right then and there how much she herself had grown in her time with Jack, mostly from their disagreements and miscommunications. It was a stone cold fact that when people speak of "growing up", the process is one that can ONLY proceed within the context of relationships, and preferably romantic ones. This explained Snacks' arrested development, as well as Isaac's and no doubt most of the other brothers.

How could one grow up if they've never had legitimate romantic relationships? Snacks never had a real girlfriend, and Isaac had a new one every month. They could never adapt or compromise with the will of another and thus they both sharpened their self-centered tools constantly. Their chests were filled with lethal narcissism and dull-as-all-hell actual human relationship skills. This continued for Stevey who married a total dictator and thus fell right into his older role of servant within the bigger brothers. Naturally, his daughter adopted the stronger partner's tendencies and shoved him deeper into his subservient role. Paul married a helpless partner that makes him feel powerful and thus he never needed to be ambitious enough to improve himself. Finally, there was Stanley who must have had his fair share of relationships. Angie had no clue, just the criticisms of his mother to fathom a guess, but he must have had more experience considering he was the most well-adjusted of the group.

The Norossi brothers had stunted their already slow growth by either dismissing romantic partners, not seeking them, or clinging to them like a puppy onto a choking hazard. This, like many other issues, probably came about in a large part because of their eccentric parents. Mama Norossi ruled like a dictator, but not in a way that required her to wield her power with force. Instead, she would rain guilt and disappointment on anyone who challenged her rulings. Bobz was powerless and he soon assumed the role of court jester as a result. Thus, each brother had to first overcome this dreadful blueprint for a marriage to make their own relationships work... and most of them failed.

Right as she began thinking about how Jack, like some of his brothers, hadn't had much experience in relationships prior to her either, she saw that she received a letter from her sister, Charlie. That very important trait of her future husband demanded a level of attention that was too much for her to process right now. Instead she opened the letter and did her best to decode her sister's handwriting.

Angie,

Thanks so much for inviting us to the BBQ at your AMAZING home. Oscar and the boys were thrilled. (Keegan and Lee keep asking when we can come back, so I hope you're ready for these boys to be swimming all summer!) Auntie Angie impresses once again. Hehe. Also, the food was great, the music was crazy good, and it was just so nice to have everyone together like that... even the Norossis. (Jk Jk)

I think everyone is already laughing at what happened. It was so silly, but it's going to be a hilarious story as more time passes. I hope you're not stressing too bad about it. I know Mama looked upset, but you know how she is with stuff like that. I told her that's just how boys are and she was spared from that stuff because she has three perfect princesses. Hahaha. Just don't personalize it and make it your fault. No one's going to hold it against you, seriously.

I hope things are better at home with "That Man". (I don't know if he reads your mail lol, so I won't say the name. That person can guess which one I'm talking about.) Let me know if I need to come over anytime and help you keep the peace or get something done. I just moved up a class in my kickboxing club so I can show you what I'm learning. Ha!

Also, Oscar is asking me again about Lakers' tickets and I promised him I'd ask you. If there's anything you can hook us up with, he'd appreciate it. He keeps saying the boys need to see as much as they can because it's more fun when you're a kid, but I know he just wants to flex that suite to his buddies. I don't even think he watches for the game; he's mainly there to stare at the Laker girls, ugh. If you see him there, keep an eye on him. Jk jk, but really.

Well, I should let you go. Please write me back ASAP. You've been lacking lately. Please vent. Tell me everything those boys do to your house. I want to sit for hours and shake my head while you tell me about dirty dishes and lifted toilet seats.

Love you lots, sis! So happy for you and your home. Get that guy to marry you and put a baby in that belly! Hahahaha

Your fave sissie,
Charlie

P.S. Give me a time and a place for lunch. I got more to talk about and I can't leave a paper trail about these subjects. Hehe.

...

Snacks had three more weeks left to find a gig and $500, and he hadn't made any progress at all. To be fair, he wasn't really trying. He was spending about thirty to forty minutes a day scrolling through the feed on job sites, maybe clicking on one here or there, and then going back to YouTube to watch muscle cars from the 1960's drag race.

Where he was really putting in the time was with Jessica. They were pretty much going out every night now and she was elated. Not only was he taking her everywhere she wanted to go and telling her everything she wanted to hear, but he was also paying for it all. She of course had no idea he was just treating this like an investment for which the return was very much worth every credit card swipe. Snacks was also being very careful during this time to not stay over every night, and no matter what, he would do some kind of chore everytime he stepped foot in her house. She hadn't said anything yet, but he was positive she noticed.

Snacks was not delusional. He knew the path toward being Jessica's live-in lover was a much easier and more realistic one than getting another job just to get kicked out at any point by Angie. The fact was his time at that house was over and any extension he could gain would always be temporary. He figured that a combination of his blossoming relationship with Jessica and the pity he would incur from being kicked out so harshly by his brother's mean girlfriend would be enough to receive a tenancy offer from her, but he wasn't quite confident enough to leave it here.

There was one more play he had in his bag of tricks, and he had a good amount of confidence in this one.

No one knew his brother Jack better than him. Snacks and Jack had always had a secret closeness that preceded them living together in their first apartment. He had always watched his shy brother's back and made sure since he was a more timid individual, that his brothers or anyone else would not take advantage of that. He was also there to spur him along when he was ready to retreat into his natural state of stasis, which of course is now about as ironic as it can get. Now, he would need to motivate his younger brother into a major change of status that he had been putting off for way too long--long enough at least for Snacks to notice. Fortunately for everyone in the household, he knew exactly how to do this.

That Friday, Jack and Angie made plans to have dinner at a ramen place near Staples Center. Late week dinners near her work were common for them, but tonight was different because Jack mentioned that he would be attending the Kings' game prior. Jack was very much still a diehard fan, but due to his immense professional responsibility, he rarely attended live games anymore. He could sneak off sometimes on a Tuesday night or any game on a Saturday, but these examples became fewer and fewer as he climbed up that corporate ladder.

Angie also hadn't been to a game, off-duty, for some time now. With her hours, she was never in a mood to spend more time at Staples, even though she really did love her work. She always felt bad turning down Jack when he asked if she wanted to go to a game, but she also recognized that he, too, declined her perpetual invitation, so it wasn't like it was only she who was being lame. Still, she lamented the fact that they didn't attend more games together. This had been where they had met, of course, and it was their most regular date spot when they started seeing each other. Now, they lived farther away, had big people jobs, and just... grew up. It was a blessing that the stars had aligned for tonight and she was more than ready to accept it.

Angie couldn't offer the suite tonight because the game was against the Toronto Maple Leafs and those boys always brought sell-out crowds of all price levels to downtown Los Angeles. Jack instead opted to sit in the lower bowl section right behind where the Kings would shoot twice, which was his favorite spot because he liked to share the goalie's view and he felt that this viewpoint was more akin to a hockey player as opposed to the side view of a spectator. Angie promised to meet him after she was done with her last meeting at some point in the second period and she would do her best to watch the third with him. He assured her that she need not worry and when he arrived, he made his way to his seat post haste.

As the second period got into gear, the Kings scored a big power play goal to take a 3-1 lead. Jack stood up to cheer the players and had to bite his tongue not to compulsively explain to the stranger next to him the intricacies of how that play had been set-up from the hard check in the left corner and it was actually the ability to keep tired penalty killers on the ice that really showed how far the Kings had come this season.

When he grabbed his seat again, he looked around at the different tunnels to see if he could find Angie and sure enough, there she was just like so many years ago. He looked at the tunnel just above the Kings' bench and saw the lights reflecting off that chestnut hair he knew so well. Nothing had changed. He once again fell into a daze staring at his beautiful Angela. There she was, just being her and being perfect. In this moment, time stopped and he felt her warmth across the arena. This was the woman of his dreams. This was the person he wanted to mother his children. He really, truly, honestly wished to spend every last moment with this being and shun every other female for the rest of time just to prove to her how much she meant to him. As if she could sense these thoughts, she looked over, finally noticing him, and waved. She tried to mouth her message while she pointed to her watch and held up three fingers to indicate that she would be there at the start of the third period. He smiled and nodded back, realizing that he was probably weirding her out because he was on the verge of tears in his admiration of her beauty and she would have no context as to why he was behaving this way. Jack's stare lingered as he fell back into deep thought, during which he missed the Leafs score their second goal.

The third period arrived and Angie made her way to the seat. She quickly hopped up the stairs and sprung into the spot next to Jack, kissing him on the cheek without delay. When she pulled away, she nearly wept at the fact that Jack had a cold Budweiser waiting for her. She took a big sip, settled in, and enjoyed the time off with her love.

After a few minutes of nail-biting puck, Jack said, *Do you recognize this section?*

Yeah, it's where you always sit. Because of the goalie view.

Yeah… but what else happened just outside here?

Angie paused as if it were a trick question. *Are you talking about when we met?*

Yeah! You were right in that tunnel the first time I saw you, he said trying to not appear as if he was rushing and definitely trying not to get caught gazing up at the play clock.

Oh yeah. I obviously remember that. I thought you meant something else.

Jack did his best to control his heart rate as he thanked god that the game was so good it was holding her attention and keeping it from his sweaty, blushing face. He continued: *It's so great to watch a game live together, huh? It's been forever.*

I know! I was thinking that when you texted me. We gotta make this a regular thing again. This is the best. It's like when we just started dating. The Leafs nearly tied the game just then and Angie took another big swig of beer as she complimented the tender's prowess in stopping the shot. Jack looked up and saw that the game stoppage would definitely lead to a TV timeout, and that meant this was it. As the in-arena host began to speak, he took the deepest breath of his life.

He called her name and she turned around, right away noticing how sweaty he was. *Oh my god, Jackson, are you okay?* she asked with genuine concern. This once again worked in his favor because it distracted her from what the host was saying and from the fact that the camera was now on the two of them. Jack stood up, which triggered Angie to do the same. He now took the biggest gulp of his life and said:

Angie, I love you. I don't know how I lived before I met you and I don't ever want to know how I'd live without you. That day, right here,

142

when I first spoke to you was the start of the rest of my life. You can never know what you've given me. The confident, successful, happy man that I am today is all because of you.

By this point, Angie had entered full shock, still not even noticing that 16,000+ were watching her reactions. This was it. This was the moment she was waiting for and as he fell to his dominant knee and dug into his pocket, she was transported into a dream world. It was all so perfect. This was where they met, where they had had so many conversations getting to know one another, where they really connected and forged the foundation of their relationship. Now, this was the place where they'd take that first step in the next part of their lives.

Angela Genevieve Saccomanno... will you marry me?

Jack would have preferred a quicker reply, but after an extended moment of awe, his love said yes and the whole stadium erupted. They even brought about a few stick taps from the players on the ice, which both of them would be sure to mention every time they told this story. She slipped on the handsome ring and embraced him in a monster hug she wished would last forever. They sat back down and held hands for the duration of the game, even when her co-workers had brought down a bottle of special Champagne. They toasted with the people in their section and smiled as wide as they ever had as the Kings added another goal and sent the Leafs home without even a point to show for their efforts.

•••

The next few days were a blur of phone calls, emergency lunch gatherings, and social media posts. Angie was of course not the type to hire a photographer for a special photoshoot, although she did think about how cool it would be if they did something on the Staples Center ice. Anyway, she made the required rounds and informed everyone about her engagement, and was more than happy to tell the story dozens and dozens of times in intricate detail.

She took extra joy in telling her mother, who earned a private meeting just for the occasion. Mama sat at her favorite table at the little Italian bistro she loved so very much as her youngest finally told her that she was to be married. A little of the fun had been spoiled though because Mama was so astute, she immediately asked why Angie had worn gloves to the occasion and then would not let it go when her daughter fired out flimsy excuse after flimsy excuse. Any way it went down, the fact remained that Angie and Mama had finally gotten what they wanted.

Naturally, Mama went on to pressure her about the exact date and how important it was to set one as soon as possible so it becomes real in everyone's minds and the process will have a definitive due date. Then she went on to talk about children, showing no tact whatsoever, but all that was fine because it all meant that her mom was assured that the next major life steps would follow suit and that her youngest daughter was finally growing up. She had taken that worry away from Mama, and that might have been the best part of it all.

On the other side of the house, Snacks was actually working against taking any steps forward in his life. He had succeeded with aplomb in convincing Jack that he needed to marry Angie as soon as possible. All he had to do to get him to the jewelry store was make his case for how Angie had been seeming on edge lately and with the combined stress of her work, her empathetic absorption of Snacks' troubles, and the growing impatience of her desire to marry and have kids, she was liable to lash out. He told his younger brother that he had seen this before and it never ends well. He reckoned she was liable to do something drastic like finding a new lover, flat out leave, or possibly even worse, just suffer in silence, internalizing all that anguish with the belief that she had no one to turn to. Of course, Jack was not about to let the love of his life escape and he sure as hell would not allow her to suffer needlessly on his account. Snacks then went on to tell him that

144

any distrust he was mining with her right now would bear horrible yields later in the relationship, so he best act now and assure her that she is the only one for him *'til death do they part*.

Jack indeed acted fast and actually went out to buy a ring that next day. The following Friday, he proposed. Snacks was ready with a bottle of expired-rack sparkling wine next time he saw the couple, but withheld from the bride-to-be the key fact that he had spurred the action. He needed that gem of information for later, in case Angie was still adamant on having him vacate her house in under three weeks time. Snacks remained patient in waiting for the subject to come up again, doing his best to find the exact time when she was still overcome with joy, but not so suddenly that she would suspect he was using her emotions against her. It definitely required a surgeon's precision, but Snacks had been here many times before and nearly every time, he had found that margin where everyone believed they came out ahead.

In the meantime, he continued his romancing of Jessica. This too was going about as well as it could. Snacks had the reputation of being a selfish manipulator, but one must admit that he does well in creating scenarios where everyone can prosper. Sure he lies, sneaks, and outright bullies others to his will, but most of the time it's all with gold-plated intentions.

If he succeeded with his schemes, he could find a way to secure himself a place to live, give Angie her marriage, avoid upsetting Jack, and give Jessica the life partner she was so desperately seeking.

The only issue that he wasn't ready to admit was that he had no idea how long the Jessica thing would last. (The fact that he spoke of his relationship with her as "The Jessica Thing" spoke volumes.) If he was honest with himself, he had no desire for a partner. He had no desire for friends. And he definitely had no desire for kids. Snacks just wanted to be himself and worry as little as possible about others in general. This wasn't in a Scrooge or Grinch kind of way, but he wouldn't really mind building himself a life like either of those guys.

People are inherently complicated. Everyone wants different things, and the pursuit of each one sometimes requires entirely divergent tactics. It was all so much to think about, even though quite ironically, Snacks was a master at giving people what they wanted, or maybe at just wearing them down until they changed their minds and were convinced that they wanted what he wanted. His main goal was to stay in that Norossi-Saccomanno home as long as he possibly could, but if absolutely necessary, he just hoped that he could keep The Jessica Thing going for a while after Angie kicked him out and if it ended up lasting his whole life, he guessed he would just deal.

…

Bee!

I just finished *The Supermarket Stare* and I LOVED it! You are the QUEEN of steamy romances! When Laurie and Kevin get caught about to kiss in that store's changing room… that line, "She felt the coarse, worn seams of the denim as she searched for a loop, a waistband, anything to pull him closer." I swear to god, I was sweating. Haha! And the ending, too! Wow. I knew Kevin was obsessive, but to see him go all that way for her was so crazy. I swear from like page 200, I just kept reading for hours until the end. I will definitely be recommending this to everyone at work and I'll flood your Goodreads page with positive reviews. Gotta get in there early before EVERYONE starts calling it a classic.

Jack and I discussed the wedding a little more this week and like I told you on the phone, we're definitely headed toward a spring date. April sounds good, but we need to be clear of Charlie's birthday, because you know she'll flip. It's all so far off, but so close at the same time. I'm already stressing. I'm so glad I have two sisters to help me and who actually enjoy helping. I know I had the time of my life being with you through your planning. I mean, it wasn't MY big moment so I obviously was more gung-ho. Now I know how stressful every single little detail can be. My bad if I wasn't understanding enough with you.

Anyway, we'll have lunch soon with Charlie and maybe spend a good amount of time working through some ideas: themes, colors, venues, etc. I would love your guys' help on that so much. Typical baby of the family, having two guinea pigs before she does anything. Haha. Seriously, I love you both so much and can't wait to do all this with you!

As for the other Norossi brother, he's been a little too nice lately. I'm starting to think he thinks that I'll let him slide on our agreement because I'm so happy Jack proposed. I know he thinks he can weasel his way out of anything, but he's <u>gone</u> on the first if he can't pay. That's not even my worry though, I think he's using that girlfriend of his and I don't know what lies he's telling her. I haven't met her, but I can only imagine the amount of brain damage it would take for a person to willingly date him. Of course, I'm sure he's only showing her what she wants to see so I can't really blame her for whatever happens. He says she's divorced so I hope she's not one of those lonely doormat types. I know what you're gonna say about not being everyone's savior, but it still bugs me. I would hate to think that me finally getting him off our back is just forcing him onto hers. I'm really trying not to think about it.

Well, that's all I got for today. Please let me know how Ariana's ballet classes are going. I can't wait to see her in her little tutu on stage next month! And please give me an update on your podcast! I'm dying to subscribe when it launches. If you try to back out of it, I'll smack you! Haha. I'll even be a guest! Seriously, your books are not enough, the world needs your voice!

Love you lots always, sis!

-- Angie

•••

The rude awakening of Snacks Norossi would happen on an abnormally rainy summer day in Southern California. It was also a rare occasion where the temperature dropped under sixty degrees. He had about ten days to pay his $500 rent (and get a job) and it was clear to all parties involved, he wasn't going to make the cut. Snacks was smart enough to know that he should at least address the matter now so he could change course if need be, and he knew that he should address Angie directly because she valued that kind of initiative and would also be pissed if he tried to negotiate with Jack behind her back.

Snacks woke up at about 13:10 and made his normal path toward the fridge to take a swig of his cow's milk, straight from the jug. Jack was on the living room couch torturing himself by watching the Angels' bullpen blow another lead to an awful Oakland team, while Angie sat doing some work on her laptop at the table just behind him. Snacks had long stopped his 'mornin' greeting and replaced it by simply criticizing something at hand and starting a rant/conversation from there. In this case, he led with a condemnation of the Halos' pitch selection, which he said was because "those jokers were afraid to challenge the bats". As he said this, he took a moment to read the room and saw a favorable environment to skillfully inquire about the housing situation. Jack looked immersed in this game and Angie in her work. He noticed that although she was still basking in the joy of her engagement, the thrill was just beginning to cool because she was going back to her workaholic default--at least enough to miss an Angel game. The time was now.

Snacks lowered his voice a bit and started with Angie, *They got you working on the weekend, huh?*

Yeah, it's a group we got together to talk about promotions for next year, and they're all over the place. Some want punk music nights, vegan nights, crazy socks nights. I have to summarize it all and give a recommendation on what should move forward.

Just tell them to watch the damn game, Snacks laughed.

That's what I say. She trailed off, which pleased Snacks because it further proved that she was very much absorbed. There were two ways to look at this. Either she was busy and any discussion would annoy her, or she would be so into her work that she would be more apt to agree to things without much clarification. Distraction was his best friend at the moment and he was about to see just how far this friend could take him.

Yeah, I shouldn't even talk. I'd kill for someone to give me some weekend work right now.

No luck on the job search, huh? she responded without looking up from her laptop.

Naw, I was talking with Mick the other day and he said they needed some guys at his brother-in-law's moving company. You know my back's all shot, then with this UTI, I gotta be careful with anything strenuous, but I told him to set it up. Then get this. The guy calls me up last night and says that business has been so slow that they're actually laying guys off now. Can you believe that? Sometimes you can't catch a break, you know?

Sheesh. You'd think that would be a safe business. People always need movers. With this she sat back in her chair and looked him in the eye, much to his chagrin. For that beat, he almost felt a touch of rage. But then he met that emotion head on and thought to himself: Why did she scare him so much? He wasn't afraid of anyone, yet he was over here dancing on egg shells for her. She was just a normal woman--an Italian woman, so definitely stronger and more intense than normal--but really just a person.

Was it the power? The fact that she had gone toe to toe with him and put her foot down had surprised him, sure, but contrary to popular assumption, he had, in fact, heard the word "no" before. Then again, he had never been threatened with eviction, and certainly never when he had pretty much no other place to go. He also hadn't been unemployed since High School, so he was no doubt feeling more than a little emasculated by that. Combine that with the fact that he lost that job trying to get on Angie's good side, and he started to put the puzzle together.

As she looked at him with her intensely direct brown eyes, he wondered who this was. Why had she entered his life? He knew she wasn't going to budge on the rent. She hadn't budged on anything. He was good enough to get her to give him extensions, but he would have to pay. He should have paid earlier because if he did, he could have milked those dollars at least a little. Right now she had a lot of clout riding behind the fact that he hadn't contributed even one cent to the homeowners his entire stay. Snacks knew well that Angie was one of those money types who only judged you by how much cash you could contribute. No way she would have said yes to a date with Jack if he had been broke. This wasn't a negative thing about her, but it wasn't a positive either.

Snacks was not known for being especially self-aware, but anyway he wanted to look at it, the fact was that he was trapped here. He had no way out. He couldn't find a job and he definitely didn't have $500 to give her in about a week and a half's time. He would have to move in with Jessica. At this point he had no other choice than to ask her to let him move in instead of asking Angie for an extension. Angie was a tough cookie, and he finally had to admit--perhaps for the first time ever--he didn't have the strength to break her. To put it bluntly and maybe even crossing into unfairly, he needed a new host for his parasitic ways.

His facade softened and he dropped his eyes from Angie's. *Yeah, I'll find something though*, he said as he made his way back to his room, as defeated as he had ever felt in all his wasted years on this floating rock. He closed the door, locked its loud latch, and grabbed his phone.

He dialed Jessica and asked her if she was free to hang out today. She was.

...

It was a fuzzy memory, but Snacks remembered a specific moment when he was around ten years old and he saw his father talking with his mother. Bobz and Mama Norossi were in their kitchen screaming at each other about something or other. Obviously, he didn't understand the specific adultspeak and thus his memories were more noises and foggy images than anything else.

His mom's tone grew higher in pitch as the argument progressed and Bobz' voice grew louder. Back in this early stage of his marriage, Bobz was not so afraid to challenge his wife. It was years of losing argument after argument and finally receiving divorce papers, then having to deliver a hefty settlement that finally reduced him to the shell of man that he was today. Combine that with a crop of sons that never could respect him for letting their mother walk all over him, while at the same time always siding with her and ganging up on him, and one can understand his plight. This was extra depressing when it was abundantly clear to anyone with a decent amount of empathy that all Bobz ever wanted was to get his sons ready for the world by instilling in them the discipline necessary to do so and he was shut down at every turn by their mother who always loved her children thousands of times more than she ever loved him.

Anyway, on this particular evening, Snacks' parents shouted and screamed until Mama Norossi began vehemently stomping her feet and Bobz backed off. His voice dropped in volume and he began to slow his cadence. Mama Norossi continued to screech and Snacks saw his father wipe his brow in frustration. As an adult now, he knew that this was the kind of frustration every man must deal with often in his life. His opponent was not going to see his point of view no matter how hard he tried. There was no argument to be had because it was only a matter of who would back down first. This was not a discussion. It was war. Snacks, much like his father, did not see that they were both doing the exact same thing as their respective opponent and were thus just as guilty a party to the frustration as their rival was.

If Bobz had seen this, he might have been able to take a step back and try a different approach. Instead, he suffered by his own hand and continued to pick at the wounds of his marriage. Of course, he was unaware just how fast those wounds would infect, then annihilate the marriage entirely, and even more unfortunately, the union wouldn't wither fast enough for Bobz to salvage whatever self-respect he still harbored.

Mama Norossi got so angry at this point that she scooped up her son and stormed out. Snacks was happy to be in his mother's arms, as he always was, and couldn't understand the look of pain and sadness on his father's face as he was carried out and into his mother's car. The trip was fantastic for him because all she did was tell him how much she loved him and how special he was and how he was lucky because she would make sure he wouldn't be anything like his father. He would be a strong man. He would make lots of money and treat a woman like a queen. He would be the big boss at his work and all his influential friends would look up to him for being so brave and smart and handsome and strong.

Mama took him to McDonalds and let him get all the ice cream he wanted. She bought him three happy meals, just so he could get one of each toy. Once again, she told him about how lucky he was that he looked just like her dad, who was the most beautiful man she had ever known. She said how she missed him so dearly and every time she saw Snacks' face, she was so happy because it was like he was back here with her. She must have told the child that she loved him a thousand times that night before taking him back home and tucking him into bed. She kissed the unconscious boy on his forehead about a dozen times before she told him she loved him once more.

Snacks liked this memory a lot.

...

Of course Angela was thinking about children despite having just been proposed to less than two weeks prior. She had been thinking about them from the first time she saw Jack smile and had her imagination hijack her train of thought to a place in the future where a much smaller version of him would show that exact same smile with that precise location of the dimple over his left cheek. The ring just made those fantasies more realistic.

By that same token, she was just as reluctant to bring up the subject with Jack, especially when he still had time to run away. She instead internalized the thought about how she was set to convert Snacks' bedroom into a nursery, so much so that she already had an Amazon wishlist of related goods worth over $5000. It was now one week until their agreement came to terms and he hadn't spoken a word to her about any progress. He hadn't spoken to her about anything actually. She hadn't seen him in days.

She figured it was only right to assume he wasn't going to make it and had instead shifted his efforts into finding a new place to live. She was also not a complete idiot so she knew the process wouldn't be as clean as she was depicting. Snacks would no doubt have something up his sleeve and she was prepared to handle whatever tactics he would employ. Why should she be afraid? She was engaged to his brother now and if need be--if ABSOLUTE need be--she would make good on her threat and tell Jack that Snacks must vacate, or she would. The engagement only strengthened her position.

Angela was, above all, a strong woman. She loved Jack with all of her heart, more than anyone had ever been able to draw from her, but the truth was that a life partner was useless if she lost her sanity and joie de vivre in the process. She had already been drained of too much already.

A few days later, Snacks sent a text. It went to both Jack and Angie. He needed to meet.

Snacks had never gathered anyone together and Angie was rightfully nervous. This was what she had been anticipating. He was surely going to make one last-ditch effort to stay in the household. She just didn't know what that would be. Would he scream? Would he get violent? Would he cry and beg? Her mind ran rampant with a rumpus of speculation that she tried to force back into the darkest parts of her mind where they originated. The fact remained that she held all the power and she wasn't going to sacrifice any of it for anything. She would die by this sword if necessary.

As she sat down with Jack, she peeked over at him. In an imperfect world, this would be the moment where she would have to choose herself over him. It was unlikely, but there was a possibility that these next moments could unfold in a way where she would lose everything she had built over the last few years.

At the moment, Jack didn't seem bothered and that was for the best. He was probably more worried about how his brother would support himself if he was indeed going to vacate, but he was the alpha after all and Jack had faith that he wouldn't struggle too much to adapt. It seemed that Angie was the only one who felt the need to worry herself over any of this.

Snacks got home what felt like immediately and he set down his bag of groceries in the kitchen. As was his habit, he went to the store every day like a little old lady in a small Italian village and bought that day's groceries instead of just stocking up for a week at a time like most

Americans. As was also his habit, he brought a bag of donut holes with him and offered them to Angie and Jack.

Had to crank my car a few times this morning, he mumbled. *Been giving me trouble all week.* The fact that he started with a statement designed to invoke pity concerned Angie immensely. She kept her poker face and let Jack respond.

How many miles does it have? Gotta be close to 200 now, right?

Shit. The only reason it's still running is because I took such damn good care of it. You ever see these models on the street anymore? No way.

He continued to put away his groceries as Angie sat silently. He did the thing where he took a big sniff, like he's trying to clear some mass of body fluid from falling out of his nose by snorting it up to the more horizontal canals near his brain, then he said:

Hey, so no big deal but I just wanted to tell you guys something. That's why I texted. He put the last of the stuff away and closed the cabinet. Reaching for a donut hole out of the bag, he just casually let out: *Jessica's pregnant.*

Angie faded away as she overheard the conversation continue with words like *knocked up* and *accidental*. Raphael Norossi was going to be a father. A grown man named "Snacks" was going to be given the reins to a family. Was... was this a tactic? Was he doing this to punish her? Was he doing this to punish Jessica?

The rest of that talk was a blur, but she did hear him say that he would be moving in with Jessica very soon. He said something about how it was kind of perfect in a weird way and she might have imagined this next part, but maybe he even spoke about how it was about time he lived in his own place. The more she thought about it, the more she couldn't imagine that he would call Jessica's apartment "his" place, but that was beside the real issue.

Angie would never in a billion lifetimes claim that an absence of a father hindered her life in any way... but it did, significantly. She hadn't only been deprived of 50% of a traditional parental unit, but more

155

importantly, she had seen how the excess pressure of parenting forced onto her mother had made her cold, suspicious, and above all, highly judgmental. Angie was the youngest so she naturally didn't see as much of the devolution from when her father left the picture, but her sisters spoke of it often. She loved her mother more than anything, but she was highly flawed and her toxicity was contagious to the point where even her daughters had to limit their time with her.

Since Angie had only known the colder version of her mother by virtue of her birth order, she had to withstand a much harsher and meaner matriarch than her sisters had. Once again, she wouldn't admit it, but this had made her suspicious on a higher level than her siblings. This is most likely why she took longer to find a suitable partner, and why when she did, she was always so afraid he would change his mind and leave at any moment. Without diving into a strictly psychological profile of Angie, the absence of her father left its mark.

If she had been the reason that Snacks found it necessary to use Jessica as his next host, thereby creating the exact same situation that had stunted her own growth and robbed her mother of her personality... she didn't know what she would do with herself.

There was no going back now. Snacks had made the last-ditch effort she had feared, but it wasn't an act against Angie, at least not directly. It was an act against Jessica and the unborn child. They would have to pay for Angie's stubbornness. She couldn't stand a few boxes on the floor of her precious little home, and now a little girl would have to grow up with Norossi blood in her and she would have to be very lucky--or maybe the reverse was true-- for Snacks to even stick around long enough to fill his fatherly role at least partly.

And this thought led to the most troubling of all.

Wasn't Angie already thinking about replacing Snacks' room with a room for her children? Wouldn't her own children have half Norossi blood? They wouldn't have the same makeup as Snacks, but they would have roughly the same seeds. They would also have the same Gualtieri genes that made up her own father. Was she actually becoming

156

excited with having a child that would ultimately become a worse combination of two of the most narcissistic, monstrous men she had ever known?

The worst part of all of these thoughts hitting her at once was that she had no refuge with which to contemplate them. Of course, this in turn added to the trauma because she should have had that refuge in Jack. So, she ended up having to do something she hadn't remembered doing since she was a teenager. She locked herself in the bathroom and just sat on the floor. If nothing else, she had the space away from everyone else and as painful as the loneliness was that she felt that very moment, the last thing she needed was for anyone to infringe on that isolation.

...

Dear Mama,

Tomorrow is finally the day! Raphael has already moved a lot of his stuff out of our house and he's been sleeping at his girlfriend's apartment pretty much every night since he told us he was leaving. Obviously, I'm very relieved even though I know the move is going to be a pain if it's anything like when he moved in. I can't tell you how much I regret not taking your advice. I keep saying it, but you need to just slap me next time I do something dumb like that. I'm sure the Good Lord will punish me accordingly and give us a daughter that will LOVE to rebel and go against everything I try to tell her I already learned the hard way.

Anyway, the deed is all but done and I promise you we will NEVER, EVER let anyone live with us like that again. (The door is always open to you, of course).

It will be so nice with the house to myself. It'll finally be like it's MY house, as sad as that might sound. AND, maybe the best news of all: you can come have dinner, watch movies, play games, and all that stuff, and you won't have to worry about getting home late because you can sleep over! We're going to put a (clean) bed in that room ASAP and make it a little guest room, and you're welcome anytime!

I can't remember the last time we had a sleepover now that I think about it. Guess that's a blessing because the only reason that is, is because we live so close to each other. Sometimes I think we take that for granted so much, even though we see each other all the time. I don't know if you noticed amidst the hoopla at the BBQ, but Jack's mom was staring at his brother Stanley all night. I can't imagine how much it hurts to have her child live so far away, and she must know he doesn't particularly want to visit, so that can't help. Part of that is her fault, but still. I just think it would be so hard to move away from you and the girls. To be honest, I kind of thought about it. Every once in a while I'll get an offer to work for some east coast team or something and I think about taking Jack with me to get away from his family. I know that sounds bad, but you were at the BBQ. Now that we're engaged, I'm thinking about our kids and I don't want them to fall into this line. Not that it's the worst line, but it's not what I want for them. I shudder thinking about a future with all these grown men behaving like that at one of my kid's birthday parties. I was doing my best to maintain my composure through the whole debacle, but I almost lost it when I saw how close Isaac came to falling on top of Charlie's boys. I'm sure I'd end up in a jail cell if that had happened to one of my kids. Don't even want to think about it.

I've actually been thinking TOO MUCH about Snacks' future child and what kind of monster that could turn out to be. Maybe the baby will force him to grow up, but I feel like that's reaching. I'll talk to you more about this in person, but I just know how hard it was for you with us three, and I know I missed a lot not having a father figure around, even though you made that bad situation so much better for me.

I really think Jack would make an amazing father--just to be clear, and I'm NOT pregnant. He's very sweet and selfless, with me and his brothers. Sometimes it's a bad thing because he either spoils them or just enables them, but it comes from a good place. With the exception of maybe Stanley, he's very different from the others in his family. I just wonder if he's different enough. I get worried when I have to clean up all of his dishes, or when I see his laundry basket overflow. Then when I see how he can't stand up to his brothers, or how he always wants me to answer the door… I don't know, maybe I'm just old-fashioned or I expect too much. Of course, I don't even know if I'd be a good parent. Maybe all you can do is try.

Well, I'd just go on and on, so I'll stop here. You can tell this has been on my mind pretty heavy, huh? Let's get brunch, ASAP, just me and you. I promise I won't just whine and talk about my problems!

Love you Mama!
-- Angie

Angie thought about it later and decided she really should have sent that letter. Instead, she filed it away and just texted her mom about the brunch. Then when they finally gathered, she barely even brushed the subjects, so it was all for naught.

Just sitting there and writing the letter had helped, though. It was nice to see it all there in front of her. After torturing herself for a few days and throwing out countless letters addressed to Stanley and her sisters, Angie came to the conclusion that there was no clear answer to calm her doubts. There were no books to clarify, no meditations to seek, no wise elders to decide for her. Neither her sisters nor her mother, not even her fiancé's brother could help her. She had to make the call herself, and she knew from her time with Snacks that she needed to make it as early as possible.

VACANT

The day was finally here. It was an exceptionally bright and warm day, and it only grew warmer into the afternoon when Snacks packed the last of his boxes into a truck Jessica had rented. These were the same infamous boxes he had moved in with, which ironically were once again, the last thing to be moved. Angie noted the faded "S" on each one. He had been too lazy to write his entire nickname.

Unlike the move-in, he had actually already moved the majority of his stuff. Of course, Jack had helped, but Snacks took the lead. He even used his own car for the trips and he never asked for gas money. This was about as bittersweet as it could get because this was the Snacks she would have loved to see on their move-in--or at any time during his residency, but much like Jana Kramer famously sang, it became apparent that Angie got the "boy" and Jessica would get the "man".

Snacks even told them that they didn't need to help him unload at the new place. He had a bit of a drive to North Hollywood and he knew he would hit some traffic so it didn't make much sense to drag them along, too. They had never known him to have such foresight in anticipating traffic.

Fortunately, the Norossis didn't have a sentimental bone in any of their bodies so the goodbye was short and sweet. Even though this would be the first time in quite a while that Jack and Snacks would not live together, they marked the occasion with a quick, *See ya.* Snacks hopped into the driver's seat, then waved and sped off.

Again, Angie couldn't help but compare that day with their move-in, which was one of the most traumatic days of her life. Now, it was nothing but peace and quiet. The street was deserted and Jack didn't say a word. The truck had driven out of sight and they both stood on the sidewalk staring at where it had turned. She looked over at her fiancé and saw that he was indeed a tad melancholy. He loved his brother dearly--that was no secret--and now he only had Angie, just like she now only had him.

She grabbed him by his hand and led him inside. They quickly realized that the quiet would take some getting used to. There was no slamming of the bathroom door, nor loud clicking of his old bedroom lock. No microwave beeps. No one came in to turn on the TV, hike up the volume, then just leave. The silence had become the most foreign and uncomfortable sound they had ever heard in that house.

Angie always wished she had kept a journal. Her head was often overwhelmed with persistent thoughts of all kinds and she believed that if she just put some of these down, she could return to them later and, with a clearer head, address the issues. Unfortunately, that thought itself would remain persistent, because she never actually started writing one.

Right now, her head was flooded with thoughts about her home and what that word even meant to her. She knew being a homeowner was the foundation of adulthood and how one kept one's home said a great deal about themselves. Where they chose to live, what architectural style, the interior design; it all spoke volumes about its inhabitants. Yet nothing spoke more than the inhabitants themselves.

Obviously... Snacks had been the signature resident, as is common with the one that makes the most trouble.

Her house was by all means bedlam with two Norossi boys running the show. It was an unbridled and berserk activity that never really stopped. It just so happened that every residents' work hours layered and thus there was almost no quiet time in the house. Imagine what it would be like if someone had a Big Brother-type feed on the three. Viewers could just sit for days watching them move in and out, arguing, faking smiles, and making everyday concessions just to keep co-existing.

With the situation now, it would be the most docile and boring feed on the internet. There was no more Snacks. There were no more epic living room battles. There was only Angie, often just sitting at the dining room table, twirling her the tip of her finger onto her laptop's trackpad with an empty stare. The audience wouldn't even have the ability to be entertained by the conflict in her head. How she pondered her future. How she hated herself for even thinking about leaving Jack.

How she hated herself even more for considering staying with him at the cost of her children's development, or the lesser cost of her development. On an even deeper level, the audience would never even sniff how she would at one point think that kicking Snacks out was the worst thing she could have done. In his own strange way, he was the adhesive between her and Jack, and in many ways, the entire Norossi family. Whether this was a good thing or just a powerful and ultimately unsustainable compensation was an entirely different issue.

The days went on and the fact that Jack didn't notice at least enough to comment on his fiancée's downtrodden mood was indication enough that her concerns were valid. He went about his business as usual, joining her for dinner most nights and even still meeting at a spot close to Staples Center on Fridays. They never made good on their vow to attend more Kings' games together, but Jack figured it was just too hard after all and never pressed the issue. Angie had waited in vain for him to bring it up the entire time.

...

Winter in Southern California is only hard for native Southern Californians. They're the only ones who would wrap up their necks in scarves and pack their ears under beanies the moment it drops under 65. Angie herself was notorious for breaking out her sweaters in late September, receiving her fair share of jabs and roasts from her coworkers as she complained that the air conditioner was on far too high for its purpose of simulating clement weather.

It was only a few days until Christmas and the office was giddy with holiday cheer, which was very much necessary because all Staples Center-hosted teams were in full force. Christmas was by far the busiest part of her year and this was proving to be no exception as ticket sales were way down and whispers of heads rolling were just starting to be heard throughout the hallways.

The stress of being fired from her dream job through no fault of her own and solely on the team's failure to get their shit together and win some damn hockey games was actually a welcome shot of flavor to her life at this time. The pressure required her to spend more time at work, take more meetings, interact more deeply with fans, and ultimately make her job her entire life now, instead of just most of it.

It was also a busy time at the firm for Jack with a ton of accounts needing to be processed before everyone slowed down for Christmas break. He would often not get home until after 01:00, allowing Angie to settle in, unwind, and fall asleep as if she lived alone. There were even stretches of days where they didn't see each other at all. A quick text here or there was all the contact they had. This was fine with both of them as they were so preoccupied, but Angie was still carrying her overwhelmed mind with her at every turn and the lack of seeing her lover and his apparent nonchalant attitude about it kept her doubts swirling.

Although she had felt the harsh isolation that came with the decision of taking sole responsibility for the direction of her life, she did have one pair of ears, or eyes, that she could reach out to. It was no easy task, but Angie swallowed her pride and decided to break out her stationary and seek the counsel of truly the most experienced, and fearless, in the arena of massive life-changing moves. The one she had almost forgotten:

Dear Stanley,

Your last letter was a lot...
But I'm very happy you sent it.
Just an update: Snacks is finally out. He's with his
baby mama now (not sure if you heard) and hopefully
he'll be able to find work soon. Our house is so quiet
now, it's eerie. I grew so used to the slamming of the
microwave door and the late night potty breaks he would

take… with the door open so I could literally hear the stream. (There are much worse examples as you can imagine.)

So… I might as well be as honest with you as you were with me. Well, first of all, another update in case you hadn't heard: I said yes to marrying Jack! I had wanted to marry him from our earliest dates--as soon as I started to really know him and that feeling only confirmed as we kept dating. It was so perfect too, how he proposed. I'll have to send that story later. I said yes right away and now it's official.

Jack is definitely like you, and neither of you are like your brothers, at all. I remember when I saw you at the BBQ-turned-debacle, I knew it was you right away not just because I had seen the few pictures you were in, but you were so different, you immediately stood out--in a good way, of course. Every time I talk to one of your brothers--any of them--I start thinking that maybe Jack isn't actually related. (Outside of his thick Norossi hair haha.)

Honesty again: I do really worry about marrying into the family. You handled it so well though, it gives me hope. I mean, I have my own personal family issues that I worry about, too. To be brief, my father had substance abuse issues and I don't even remember him because he disappeared when I was a baby. It was almost worse than him just OD'ing or something because I don't even know if he's still alive. I also can't ask my mom about it because she gets very guarded if I even brush the issue, which is hard on multiple levels. She was very distant from her own family and I think the situation with my father was part of it, so that means I have no one that can give me any more info, outside of my oldest sister who says that she can't remember anything about him dying, but she does remember our mother talking to her mother on the phone and speaking about how he had left so abruptly and she was worried so much about what she was going to do with three little girls. So as you can see, the Saccomannos aren't the cute little warm and close Italian-American family, either.

I did figure that you moved away from everyone for a reason. I know it must have taken a lot of strength to break from your family, even if they were overtly toxic like that. I don't know if I could be as strong, although the fact that I've been thinking about it so much lately makes me think I'll find out soon enough. Obviously I don't want to live away from my sisters and mother... but part of me does want that distance. I'm sure you can relate. Also, I don't even know how Jack would react to me asking him about that. He's been so busy and getting so many big accounts lately, I wouldn't even want to worry him, but if this is something, I need to talk to him before we "seal the deal". Just writing that made it seem so permanent. Yeesh. Guess it doesn't have to be, though. You found something great, but if you didn't, you could've come back... but maybe that was like the worst case scenario itself.

I really do admire you for the life you've built. You've had to really be decisive and work really hard, because your path was so far away from other people in your situation. That's part of why I like writing to you and why I was so sad to not get to talk to you in depth at the party. (Maybe some other time will come up. I need to get back to Miami!)

Hey! Maybe we'll move over there and be neighbors! Haha JK. Now I KNOW I've been writing for too long!

Thanks for reading! Sorry if I sound like a complete mess… I feel like one.

Whatever happens, I hope we remain pen pals. Really.

I'll tell Jack you said hi.

Thanks again,
-- Angie

• • •

Winter seemed especially short that year. Angie began to walk the dogs without a beanie as early as late January. She had exclusively assumed this role since Jack had been taking on later hours. He had recently been moved to a new department at his firm. It was a lateral move, but one they needed, so he made it. They had previously shared the dog walking duties ever since Snacks had left. The dogs noticed right away, especially Bella, who would often look back when they left as if she expected Snacks to come out of the house and join them. Angie's heart broke for her pet every time the pup took her pause. Snacks hadn't even said goodbye. She gave him the benefit of the doubt that it would've been too painful since he openly loved that dog unlike anyone else. She had seen Snacks embrace Bella more than his own mother, although she also accounted for the smaller sample size.

It had been closing in on seven months at this point and she hadn't even spoken to her former tenant. She thought about texting him a few times just to say hi and ask how he was faring, but she always stopped after deleting the message contents and starting over a few times. Jack only gave her brief summaries of their own sparse communications so she had nothing to really digest.

Had she not been wrestling with her own onslaught of thoughts and worries, she would have suggested to Jack to invite Snacks and Jessica over for dinner or even a double date. This was quickly abandoned when she realized that if they did agree and she saw a wartorn Jessica show up, it would only make her feel even more horrible than she already did. The risk was too high and as much as she hated choosing an option that kept her blind, but sane, she did.

In truth, Angie had made her decision. It had been done far too late, of course, and it would be a little while before she accepted that she had, in fact, made it, but it was decided.

As her head cleared coming off the trail, she wondered what Stanley would say in response to that last letter. Would he write her a long response detailing a bunch of insight and a final support of what she was trying so hard to reveal to him? She almost felt guilty for thinking about this so much because she hadn't even written about those issues to her own sisters or mother, and she knew they wouldn't be so much angry, but hurt that she had reached out to a "stranger" instead. The fact was that Stanley was the expert and she believed it was no accident that he entered her life right at this time.

Angie let Mark and Nora pull her back toward her home as she noted how well-behaved they were on their walks. They obviously weren't Norossis like Bella, who was always a handful and thus needed to be walked separate from these two. The symbiotic relationship between these two always warmed her. She didn't know specifics about their history, but she liked to think that they met in a pound as puppies. Maybe their kennels faced each other in the cold, lonely room where they were inhumanely stored and they kept their spirits up just by the fact that the other was there with them. They had no way of interacting or sharing their sufferings or fears, but just by the look across the way, they gave each other the strength to keep going. As their friends were adopted one by one, each time a young family walked in and grabbed some other dog, their hope would become not that they would get

170

adopted and removed from this steel hell, but that the other would be spared first.

Maybe one day a young boy and his younger sister entered with their parents and looked in each and every cage until they came upon Nora. The snow white coat still had its bright sheen and her deep, dark eyes were as cute as they come so it would be no surprise when both children began whining to take her home. Upon release from her kennel, she was enveloped in the warm arms of the toddler, melting the pup with a kind of mammal contact that she hadn't felt in so long. Despite being disabled by the unconditional love of her new best friend, Nora would still manage to yelp in Mark's direction, concerning the parents and the shelter owner. They would look in the direction of Mark's kennel and wonder what it was about this dog that Nora was addressing. The owner would confirm that they were not siblings and he hadn't the slightest clue to the outburst. A child would insist they adopt him too, but the parents would decline and try to hurry them along, but Nora would only yelp louder the further she was dragged. It would be the little girl who would have to flash her own puppy eyes to convince her parents that they definitely did need another dog in the household. Thus, both Mark and Nora would earn their freedom together, each being carried to their new home in the arms of a warm, loving child.

The years would go by and they would be able to form an actual friendship within the confines of their new home and with their new family. They would see the children grow into pre-teens and share in so many great times with the unit... until the failing economy would force the parents to downsize and give up the dogs for adoption. They would hardly need to fret though because Caleb, a co-worker of the father, was willing to take in both together and thus, they would continue their journey unbroken.

Of course, then the story gains more non-fiction elements as Caleb eventually would relinquish the two to Snacks, who would--without permission--agree to take them into Angie and Jack's house, and here they were, walking in front of their latest mother on their way back home, still together.

Angie always thought about the inspirational concept that whatever has tried to kill you has failed every single time so far. The problem of course with that logic was that one day something would kill you.

One day something would drive these two apart and if they were lucky, it would be death followed immediately by the other's finale. Of course, most are not so lucky and if another separation was truly forthcoming, it could very well be the one that finally drives these two bona fide soulmates in opposite directions.

As her house crept up over the hill, she noticed right away how the lawn was developing a brown spot right where it met the cement walkway. It wasn't very noticeable and most people probably walked by without even thinking about it, but it stood out so much at that moment--a straw yellow blotch on the otherwise healthy green landscape.

It was in such an odd place, too. Not where someone was stepping regularly like the path Snacks used to leave when he cut across the lawn to get his, and only his, mail. This was just a bit of slow-dying vegetation impeding the otherwise uniform greenery. She didn't know the first thing about lawn maintenance and hadn't a clue as to why a spot would form apart from the rest.   The irony of course was that this was something she would have asked Snacks to take care of, and in six months or so, he would probably fix it. Now, and maybe for the first and only time ever in her home, this problem was solely hers to solve.

She would've stopped if she had the presence of mind to fully examine what she was realizing. Instead, Mark and Nora continued to pull her closer to the lawn of her current focus as she drifted into a world where she would never address the dead patch.

In this world, she would tell Jack that she was truly sorry, but she would have to suspend the engagement and move out of this house

172

without delay, if for nothing else to decompress from this persistent onslaught of doubts and pressures.

In this world, she would have to reach out to either Charlie or Bee, probably the latter, to see if she could camp out at their place for a little while because although she could afford a temporary place to stay alone, solitude would certainly exacerbate the problem.

Yes, in this world she had now mentally landed upon and was finding more and more appealing, she would confirm that although she was incredibly in love with Jackson Norossi and in spite of the fact that she was already so behind on her life's plan to marry, have children, and just be a grownup... she would have to throw away everything she had worked so hard for and start from even less than she did before she gave that handsome, shy, and oh so genuine boy her phone number so many years ago.

This was a scary world, indeed, but the scariest part was that this world felt more like home than her current one. She had resisted thinking this way as much as she could, but now that she had been guided to these concepts, she confirmed how much sense they made.

How could Angie be expected to spend her ENTIRE LIFE with the Norossis as in-laws, much less allow her own children to demonstrate their DNA? Her presence here had been nothing but destruction and atrophy. She just put more pressure on Jack to stand up to his brothers, she pissed off Mama Norossi, worried her own mother, and now she forced Snacks to impregnate an impressionable woman with an unfathomable lack of self-worth.

The universe speaks in actions and reactions, at least according to Angie, and the reactions here were very clearly dismal.

There were only so many paces to the front door--this should only have taken thirty seconds tops--and yet she had had ample time to awaken herself to this truth. Her life needed a big jolt of change at the expense of... well, everything. Eerily enough, the process would be like how she would've addressed that blotch on the lawn. Thus identified, she would now have to speak to the right people about it, i.e. Jack, discuss the specifics of why it can't continue, possibly speak of how this came to be--at least for personal reference and avoidance of any repetition of the problem in future cases--and finally hold a briefing on what exactly the steps would be to address it. And that would be it.

He would be home around 21:00.

...

Angie always scheduled her dates firmly and for an earlier-than-usual time, especially with newer love interests. It was only their third date and she had been clear and concise that Jack should meet her at 17:00. She didn't say "sharp", but she really wanted to. She was also firm about meeting at places instead of the more traditional practice of having her date pick her up. Jack never told her this, but Isaac told him that was a dealbreaker red flag because girls who want to meet you somewhere are scared and fear leads to evil, which he probably just slapped together from a philosophical mix of Star Wars and online pick-up gurus. Needless to say, Jack paid that advice no mind.

He drove to the restaurant with his hands shaking so much that he worried he might swerve his little Prius into the next lane. Asking out Angie was one thing, but now she obviously liked him. They had a nice first date that was very, very safe with conversation barely making it past the weather and relying heavily on Kings' talk with the mandatory foray into shittalking the San Jose Sharks, the Anaheim Ducks, the Arizona Coyotes, and of course, the Toronto Maple Leafs. He had no idea how she was perceiving him and he thought all was lost when she smacked his hand away from the check at the end. She relayed to him that it was her personal code to always pay for the first date as a direct action against the sexist practice of the contrary. She said she hoped that one day the amount of women who paid on the first date would match the number of men who had, but the only way that could happen would be for a huge wave of headstrong women, like her, to take the initiative.

174

From there, she said that she had enjoyed herself and that she would "text him". Of course, he didn't actually expect her to follow-up on it and he even thought it was a sick joke when she did. She framed it very sterile by simply asking him if he saw the game the previous night. That sparked a little conversation and eventually it led to her asking if he wanted to head to a bar to watch the next game.

Thanks to the combination of a neck-and-neck contest with the Columbus Blue Jackets and the alcohol content of a few beers... and maybe a Jameson shot or two, they were able to dig a little deeper. Jack told Angie about how his dad used to sit in front of the TV watching the Lakers and Kings every night in winter, just hitting that BACK button on the remote over and over so as to miss as little action as possible. It was often only Jack who would grab a seat right by his old man and take in the excitement, always begging him to just stick to the hockey game because "those guys are cooler". Angie then hit Jack with a story about how her mom had always looked down on women playing sports, but changed her tone so fast once she saw how dominant Angie was on the diamond, and how many strangers would admire her for her unrivaled athletic ability.

Throughout the night, Jack had many opportunities to flaunt his rarely-seen humor and Angie even had the comfort with which to cuss in front of him, which is something she never did, rooted back to an instilled fear from her mother chewing her out every time she said words as tame as "heck". They continued to laugh and cheer as the seconds ticked away and the night ran on. To their mutual delight, the game extended into a few overtimes, then a shootout.

Even when they had sobered up, they both felt just as at ease with one another like they never had with anyone else. This was so extreme that Jack actually alluded to the third date himself. He told her that she HAD to try this Korean restaurant and they made a plan to mark their first of many Friday night post-work dates. If he had known there would be literally dozens more of these to come, many of which would take place right at this very restaurant, he would without a doubt have less sweat and thus more grip on his steering wheel at present.

He managed to safely park the car in the slanted spots that littered the lot and felt the immense relief as he shut off the engine and had the time to take a few breaths. He was about fifteen minutes early, which was fifteen later than he had planned, so he had to semi-rush as he collected himself.

This was a big deal. Jack knew that the third date is the crux because the rule of three is such a guiding part of everything humans do from the three-act structure of a movie to the Holy Trinity of his Catholic faith, and virtually everything in between. After tonight, they would have met on three separate occasions in three different environments and Angela would most definitely have a good idea of what kind of man he was and if he was worth the continuation of the relationship. Sure he had been impressive thus far, but tonight was the closing minutes of the game that was the courtship of his love interest.

The way Jack saw it, love was akin to basketball. This was no coincidence as to why it was his least favorite sport. Basketball's chief quality is that it is a sport where one must keep scoring and keep defending for the entire forty-eight minutes. In his beloved hockey, a team could score three seconds into the first period and then just defend for the rest of the game and win. Baseball could hold a lead-off home run, football could lock down an opening kickoff return for a touchdown, and soccer could hold onto a goal in the first minute of play. In basketball, a team could theoretically score a lay-up right after the tip-off then pitch a shutout to win, but that wasn't very realistic. Instead, the teams must try their best to score on every possession and defend on each of their opponents' possessions, because runs were bound to happen and even leads in excess of thirty points could evaporate.

When it came to girls, Jack was wise enough to realize a man must work to impress and charm on every single date. Many a quality life partner had been lost to a man due to an errant thought that his earlier seduction would serve him for an entire lifetime. Sure, Jack had played a great first few shifts, but this night was the pivot to the future. If he wanted to make Angie his official girlfriend--and in the long run, his wife--he would have to nail tonight's rendez-vous.

Upon entering the restaurant, he embraced the madness of the hustle and bustle that came with it. Petite Korean women scurried back and forth with the speed and agility of running backs, while other servers pushed stacked carts around like offensive linemen. Jack waited patiently for the hostess to return as he peered around the territory and got his bearings. He knew this place well, of course. He would never approach a moment like this on unknown territory.

As he scanned the terrain, he noticed just how busy it was on this particular occasion. This was a twenty-four hour operation and it rarely saw a lull, if ever, but there were literally no open tables at the moment. He must have just begun the wait, too, because no one else was around the hostess podium and each of the little adjacent benches were vacant.

In fact, he had so little stimulus at present that his mind wandered into its chronic anxious inclinations. He began to think about how awkward it would be if Angie showed up right now and they both had to wait like this, alone and awkward. He would have to assert himself, like a big man, and get the attention of the hostess and maybe even try a slick move, like slipping her a twenty to get seated right away. Of course, he had no idea how to do this, but he had seen it in a movie once or twice and thought it would be cool to pull it off at some point.

It was hard enough for him to talk at any point with anyone, but it would be next to impossible with an angel like Angie next to him, expecting him to step up and take care of the problem like a potential husband should. He started walking up and down the waiting area to see if he noticed the regular hostess anywhere in hopes of at least getting his name down and grabbing a seat so he could duck or something if his date came in. With no luck, he figured she might be on a smoke break and his best bet was to go outside and flag her down. For a second, he thought of just writing his name on the list right there on the podium, but then he thought she might notice the infringement and call him out on it, which would embarrass him beyond repair.

Right as he headed to the front, the door pulled open and Angie stood right in front of him, greeting him with a vibrant, hypnotizing smile. The smile soon wilted and gave way to a head tilt of concern as he tried to digest the surprise. She asked if she was that late as to have him going out to look for her and he laughed it off explaining how he needed the hostess, actually. She then pointed out that she was right there, and he turned around to see that indeed and much to his embarrassment, the hostess had returned in that seemingly split-second.

Angie had also been worrying along her drive, but for other reasons entirely . She had been thinking a lot about Jack in the days leading up to this dinner. He had charmed her right away and that was hard to do. She was exceedingly picky at this point in her life and never more so than when it came to men. He cut through all of her defenses immediately when he approached her at that Kings' game, and he had only been more charming in the moments that followed. He was funny, lively, sweet, responsible, and not a terrible looker. She was just starting to be honest with herself in admitting that she was falling for him. This had become so bad that she found herself drifting off during work just thinking about running her hands through his thick black hair or pulling down his coat to adjust it to his shoulders--neither of which she had ever done for any man.

Adding a partner to her life was not really what she was looking for at the moment and she was even surprised she had given Jack this many chances to woo her. She was right in the middle of a big project at her position that could launch her into a major pay raise and a career advancement that she had been eyeing for some time now. This would require her to spend more time at the office and at off-site activities. She had no issue with this because she had no husband or children to attend to, and her friends and family would be understanding as they always were. It was at times like these that she was able to best deceive herself into believing that she was glad she was single because it allowed her to pursue her career with extreme vigor and enthusiasm. She had not had a lover in almost two years and she always told herself that that was why she had become such a star in her department. Now, she was seeing Jack and starting to grow more and more comfortable with the idea of being his… girlfriend. Should she be worried that this will slow her momentum? Or should she be happy she found a nice guy and just play it by ear?

The answer came when she opened the door to the restaurant.

Angie led Jack back in and informed the hostess of their desire for a table. They were informed that it would be a ten minute or so wait and they accepted the terms.

The couple took a seat on the bench and Jack was surprised to find how easy it was to converse with her in what he had expected would be an onslaught of anxiety. They had picked up right where they left off and, as always, discussed the Kings' games of the past week. After taking a few final shots at the head coach, they then began speaking about Angie's job and before they knew it, they were called up and seated.

The dinner was so stereotypical as far as perfect dates go that it became nauseating--for anyone watching, not for the actual couple. They chatted incessantly, enjoyed the cuisine, had a nice drink, and just reveled in each other's company. As is common with nights like these, it had gone by so fast that both felt like they had just sat down when the time revealed otherwise.

Jack walked Angie to her car and they faced each other with nothing but a ridiculous amount of sexual tension between them. There was no way that Jack would make any kind of move this early and this publicly, so it all relied on Angie. She thought about it, but decided that she would reach in for a big hug and do her best to express how much she had enjoyed the night and all the time they had spent together so far. Of course, she would never say this out loud this early in the relationship, so she just squeezed him as hard as she could and hoped that he would understand through the intensity of the gesture.

He did not. In fact, all he could think about was how he needed to kiss her tonight because as he had researched, she was an Aries and she would quickly get bored with him if there was nothing physical developing after three long dates. Obviously, a hug did not count. He was going to get nowhere near a kiss tonight though because he was operating with about 0.00cc of confidence at this point and was honestly surprised he even made it this far in the first place. As the hug lingered, he knew he was dead to rights and since they would not share the kiss he so desperately sought, he would lose her forever. His only recourse was to hug her back with a warm squeeze by which she might remember him.

She hopped in her car and he closed the door behind her before adding a quick "See ya", which he hoped would ring as a clear message that he wanted nothing more in this chaotic twister of entropy known as life, than to see her again.

She pulled away and down the road as he stood in the center of the lane, making sure that she safely merged onto Wilshire. From there, he walked back to his car and hopped in the seat to begin his long night of overthinking the date. As he himself pulled onto the street, he believed that he could safely assume he bored her. She liked him for sure, but she was running thin on patience for his boring office talk and NHL takes. The more he thought about it, the sadder he became. He found such a perfect woman and he came close, but he just wasn't worthy enough. When push came to shove, he was a one-trick pony and a cultured, gorgeous ladder-climber like her would surely end up with some former college star quarterback who owns fifteen car dealerships and models for underwear brands on the side. He had been lucky to land three dates with a woman of Angie's caliber, and he would do his best to be forever thankful, even if he was never again destined to enjoy the company of a woman anything like her in the future.

Angela parked her car in the designated spot at her apartment and sat for a moment. She specifically requested that Jack meet her and not pick her up for this very reason. It would have been completely normal and within her right to ask him up to her room if she wanted, and she would have definitely done that if he had picked her up and dropped her off. Despite her Aries instincts, she didn't want to move too fast with a man ever and in this particular man's case, she was even more cautious. He had once again charmed her like no other and she was beginning to shift from fear of her feelings for him to warm joy at the thought of being his one and only.

Everytime she closed her eyes, she could see him look down shyly and tap his upper lip in a sort of nervous tick. His big brown eyes didn't make contact with hers often, but when they did, her stomach exploded in a barrage of butterflies and shrapnel. This was starting to go away slowly and it was being replaced by a steady obsession. (She had to stop herself twice in the next few days from setting a picture of him as her phone wallpaper.)

Angie didn't know when exactly this happened, but it had. She sat there in the quiet of night thinking about Jack and how she wasn't going to lose all her rationality just because he was perfect. However, the fact remained. Angela Saccomanno could say with confidence, even before they had shared one kiss, that she was fully and completely committed to Jackson Norossi. She wanted a future with him and already fantasized about the day he could meet her beloved Mama. (She would love the fact that he was Italian--the first she would bring home to her.)

She wasn't crazy enough to start naming their children or anything, but she did pin a few wedding dresses that night. She was still a woman, after all. The point was that she was very much looking forward to the next date and the ones after that. Soon, she would feel comfortable holding his hand, putting her head on his chest, kissing him at random, and feeling the protection under his big arms. From there, they might take vacations together, she would meet his family, and one day, maybe they would even move in together. Wouldn't that be nice?

AN EPILOGUE

The South Bay was particularly beautiful toward the tail end of summer when the heat transitioned into the coastal chill. A lot of people complained when the warmth dissipated, but Angie welcomed it this year. It wasn't that she disliked that summer, which was in no way true, but she appreciated the change. *Nothing could be worse than a climate that stood the same all year round*, she thought, blissfully unaware of how ironic it was that a native Angeleno would think this.

She sat in her condo reading her emails while one of her podcasts played, void of her attention. Living alone was something to which she had acclimated quicker than she would have predicted, but the caveat was that she always had to have some sound going whether that be music, a podcast, or the TV.

Last night, her neighbor Ophelia had come over to watch the latest episode of *Gideon's Awakening*, the hottest new premium cable series, and she had asked her to turn up the heat, at which point she realized that the pilot light was out and she didn't know how to get it back on. For a brief moment, she thought about how this problem in her old place would take the standard two or three months to be solved. Now, all she had to do was call a handyman and by tomorrow evening she would be as toasty as she saw fit.

Thoughts of the Norossi failure still crept in from time to time, especially because she had just found out that the home had sold to a new family after being scooped up almost immediately by a flipper nearly four years ago now. She tried not to be offended by the remarks she had heard about how much "work" the residence had needed to make a significant profit. Angie did her best to push those thoughts out of her head and instead focus on the work at hand.

With no such luck, she drifted her thoughts toward what she might cook for dinner. She got up and found to her dismay that she had a fridge and pantry that lacked most of the ingredients for about anything.

At least I was the one who ate the stuff, she thought, again pulled into old thoughts about Snacks and the dynamics of her previous home.

Always the wiley one, she decided that since she was out of food, it would be absolutely necessary for her to head to the grocery store right this minute to re-stock. The emails would have to wait.

The supermarket was walking distance from her place, but it was already dark and she hated the small stretch of street where there was a blind spot from the major intersection, so she just drove the half mile. This was not very practical because there was a really long red light right as she turned onto the main street and this delay often took longer than walking. As she sat in her car and waited for the red light to change, she thought about Leo, the guy she was kind of, sort of seeing at the moment. They had gone on a handful of dates that were really more like meetings. She had been introduced to him through a work friend and she had been immediately taken with how handsome he was. He was a track coach at UCLA and he had the build of a shot putter who did crossfit, as in he was about six foot four inches tall and weighed about two hundred twenty pounds with a body fat percentage that only needed one number to notate. She admitted to herself that her interest was mostly lust-based even though they had not done anything even remotely intimate yet. She liked him overall, but there was nothing really clicking and she had been wanting to find a way to tell him to essentially leave her alone, but she hadn't quite found a chance to do so.

As she entered the all-but-deserted store and made her way to the produce, her mind continued to wander to the men she had dated since her engagement imploded. There hadn't been many and none of them stuck at all. She had received a significant promotion almost immediately after she moved back to the South Bay and that had given her at least an excuse to avoid making romance a major part of her life at the moment. Of course, this "moment" had now hit multiple years so the effort in keeping up that facade was beginning to become exhausting.

After each relationship met with its end, Angie's first thought was often about how she just wanted Jackson back in that role, but she was cursed with the wisdom that being with him was incompatible with her true happiness. This wasn't one of those situations where she missed having a partner she loved and trusted. She missed Jackson Norossi and only him. She had been over this multiple times and the logic she had used to break with him always proved to be the right choice and thus, she left it at that. She was still hurt that he had cut off all communication since the sale of the house went through, but she knew she shouldn't have expected him to reach out. She broke up with him after all and whether he was pissed off, completely broken, or just found it too painful to even think about her, the result was the same: they would not be part of each other's lives anymore.

She maneuvered her cart down into the aisle holding the items she needed when she saw the first figures besides the employees she had seen all night.

She knew who it was right away, but her recognition had double-clutched and introduced doubts for some reason. She thought maybe this happened because she had never seen him in anything other than cargo shorts and a worn-out Nike hat. This man actually had pants on, too, so one could imagine why it took her so long to process who it was. This wasn't even considering the fact that he was accompanying a child, as in he was responsible for someone other than himself. Yet it was true. Standing right down that same aisle stood Snacks and his daughter, in the middle of picking between the knockoff Lucky Charms and some Disney-branded specialty release.

They didn't see her so Angie used the opportunity to observe. Once she got past the initial shock, she saw how he spoke to the child like an adult which was both adorable and hilarious. She could never imagine Snacks baby-talking anything. He was trying to talk her into picking the cheaper Lucky Charms option, but she was intent on the glittery box that cost an extra dollar. She was a loud little girl and she made her case by bringing up the limited release aspect of her choice, squeezing tightly to the box that was the size of her entire torso. Every single claim Snacks made was immediately refuted by her

185

understandably childlike hairbrain logic. Angie smiled as she imagined the countless other times that the child would torment her father in exactly the same ways he had tormented her for those brief years.

As the little girl twisted her body back and forth, her long red braids swayed recklessly and Angie tried desperately to get a glimpse of her eyes to see if they had that undersized quality of her father, or maybe she would have the beginnings of the classic Norossi forest of eyebrows just like Jack had. As she was speculating, she realized how creepy she would appear if he had turned back and seen her. To avoid that scenario, she had two realistic options from her current position: head down and say hello, or quickly escape and wait for them to leave.

She thought for a beat about how he would even react to seeing her. He might be angry with her for breaking his brother's heart, or he might take a special joy in flaunting what a great father he's become.

If she did decide to risk the reaction, she would get to better look at the product of Jessica and Snacks, and, of course, the newest Norossi (at least to her knowledge). She would also get to learn her name and get a more complete view of how Snacks behaved while being a father in front of an audience.

Angie wondered if Snacks would fill her in on what Jackson had been up to, where he was living, and maybe if he had been dating someone new. Then, he would definitely have to update her on his relationship with Jessica and what he had been doing for work. She would get to throw in some jabs about how domesticated he had become and how she would've never seen it coming. She might look at how he looked at his daughter and see, maybe for the first time, that parental stare where he would show a deep admiration and love with a shade of worry as he watched his child shyly clam up in front of a stranger.

He might even refer to her as "Auntie Angie", but she wouldn't hold her breath for that.

Snacks might say something like Jackson is finally starting to take some charge with his massive accounts and that his firm is now grooming him to become a partner. Maybe he would say that Jackson

186

moved out of his cousin's place to an apartment or home of his own and is loving the situation of just having himself to worry about. He might be meeting new people, making new connections both personal and professional, and finally getting acquainted with his loftiest goals. Maybe, he still mentions her sometimes.

Angela watched Snacks as he finally gave in to his little girl and said he would buy the more expensive cereal. She immediately started dancing with joy, a trait she definitely inherited maternally.

Angela froze even though she knew she needed to make a decision instantly. She would surely have to lie a little about her situation, even though it really didn't require any lying. She was moving on at her own pace just like Jackson was, both of which were nowhere near the pace of Snacks, apparently.

What would she say? She could lead with her career trajectory and then just do her best to brush over her relationship status. It probably wouldn't even get there. Snacks was never one to pry and now that they had almost completely reinhabited the roles of strangers, it would be even more uncouth.

However, she wondered if she half-lied and said she was single, if it would get back to Jackson. Would she even care if it did?

Would this be the last time they ever saw each other? She always thought about how she never said goodbye to Snacks, and now here he was. The chance was there. He had truly been a massive impact in her life, and not necessarily the negative one that she had believed. In fact, he was to thank for a lot of what had changed. Seeing him there with his daughter made it all so real. The universe had clearly rewarded him for playing his role.

Angela realized that in the same way, the universe would eventually reward her. She had made the right decision and all the right ones previous to the break-up. Because of her, Snacks grew up and maybe Jackson got the wake-up call he needed before he went down the same shadowy path of his older brother. She might even be so bold as to think that with the two Norossi brothers maturing, the others would follow suit. In her most self-centered fantasies, she was the agent of change that saved everyone she encountered because she was a problem-solver and a fearless action-oriented service-minded altruist.

Of course, she would never see that it was Snacks who changed her. To be fair, he would never realize it either. All she knew was that she didn't want to know any more about him or any Norossi anymore. She didn't need to. Everyone was moving forward to better things and they were all better off for having known each other, despite what they all might have felt.

Angela took a long look at the image of the father and daughter, an image that no one would connect to a stack of boxes shoved into a corner of a living room. No one would assume this man terrorized a young couple's living situation and virtually destroyed the best relationship she had ever had, and maybe ever will. And no one would ever see that he had also saved her from making what could have been the most terrible mistake of her life. They would just see a loving, caring, responsible father and his beautiful baby girl.

So, she backed up her cart silently and ventured to the back of the store where she scanned her Pinterest boards until she saw them leave.

•••

Acknowledgments

First, I'd like to thank the National Novel Writing Month organization. I don't think I'd ever sit and write something so long without some kind of structure like this challenge gave to me. Those thirty days of discipline led to what you're holding in your hands, so much thanks to the people who run that.

This being my first novel, I have to acknowledge my favorite English teachers. First would be my AP Composition instructor, Maria Goulding. She was one of the first to push me to write more prose… but I'd be so bull-headed it would take me about ten years before I finally did. Next would be my AP Literature teacher, Christine Shaw. Not only did she bring so much energy to every discussion, but she always gave me the freedom to interpret, and enjoy, the text in my own way. Finally, I'd like to thank Richard Stand who pushed me to become more disciplined with my output when I stumbled upon his playwriting class at Mt. San Antonio College. Four plays in four weeks sounded impossible, but now I write a short story each week for my podcast. It was Mr. Strand who taught me to ignore my perceived limits and just keep writing.

I'd also like to thank my parents for sacrificing so much for my education, without which I would never have met these wonderful teachers. Not to mention everything else they had to put up with w/r/t/ me…

Thanks of course to my good friend, Courtney Schehl, who was the bounce board for my ideas throughout this whole process, then she became my go-to proofreader and editor, saving me from countless spelling errors, inconsistencies, and other tells of my Gemini Mercury.

Finally, I'd like to acknowledge my Aunt Francine, whose experience working at Staples Center back in the day provided for a lot of the inside baseball that was included in the book.

About the Author

Joshua Ramirez was born in La Puente, CA. He writes short stories and stageplays with a few screenplays and now a novel, for balance. He also produces a podcast of readings of his stories entitled, *The MozzaDenza Myths*. When he's not writing, he coaches athletes in the international sport of weightlifting.

Please enjoy the following bonus short story from the author.

*The text has also been produced into an audio performance as part of Season One of **The MozzaDenza Myths**, available on YouTube and wherever podcasts can be found.*

Turn Around and Trip the Bitch

Penelope went to church every Sunday. She even volunteered with the bi-weekly trips to the food bank. After almost 28 full years of giving God more than enough glory, and putting the congregation before her own interests virtually every time, she died.

On the third day of August, Penelope and her boyfriend of five years, Denny, were driving back from a concert at the Hollywood Bowl. He was the DD. She was blasted. (It was Dave Matthews, and she always got slammed when they played. You can buy full bottles of wine at the Bowl, after all.) They made their way to the *casse-tête* that is almost any parking situation in LA, strapped in their seatbelts, and headed back to the OC. Right about the time they were making the change from the 101 to the 5, a bright blue Mercedes made contact, spun them like a little matchbox, and after a few tumbles, the two lovers reached across to grasp hands one last time as their very brief existences were expunged.

The next thing they knew, they were in a vast expanse of formless space. Well, the two of them and... Gaby*Rella. As it turned out, the world famous pop star and sex symbol was the one driving the Mercedes that night. Penelope could only assume that she was on some kind of designer narcotic cocktail at the time and it was a miracle--there was definitely better word for it--that she had made it all the way from the Hollywood nightclub to that particular interchange in one piece.

Anyway it went, Penelope, Denny, and Gaby*Rella found themselves void of their mortal coils and without a clue as to what might happen next. Naturally, Penelope was already peeved that she didn't get to die "with" her love, but in a group with him, instead. Things did not improve when GR insisted on sticking with them as they navigated the early stages of life's post script. Denny didn't mind at all. In fact, he was more than happy to share his theories on the afterlife with the gorgeous celeb--surprising Penelope because he never wanted to talk about these things during the Bible studies she always had to force him to attend. Fortunately for Penelope, before they became too comfortable, a figure appeared.

The child approached the trio, wearing nothing more than some very comfy looking jeans. He introduced himself as Matt and told them straight off the bat that they had made it! After a solid job on earth, they had earned the right to partake in paradise for eternity. He said he could answer questions if they like but since time is immaterial in the afterlife, most just dive in and figure it all out. The only thing they might want to know before they enter is that one can change to any form one likes. For example, he died when he was 98 (colon cancer) and he chose to inhabit the form of his eight-year-old self since those were what he felt were his best years. Of course, they can switch whenever they felt it--they'd soon find that "rules" weren't really a thing around here.

Still holding hands, both Denny and Penelope looked at each other and conveyed that they were fine as they were, in their sprightly, youthful forms. When pressed, GR simply stated that she had literally just had her boobs re-done so she would like to remain in present form, as well.

Penelope's church was led by a tall preacher by the name of Cutter. Reverend Cutter was beloved by his congregation, many of whom drove from miles out not only for his sermons, but also for the Bible Studies and volunteer excursions.

Cutter was a centrist in terms of his faith. He definitely spoke of hell and such, but he chose to spend the lion's share of his limited time on the pulpit speaking of the splendors of life and those that awaited the righteous in the Land of Milk and Honey. Penelope loved when he went on his streaks of explaining as best as he could the bliss that was eternity with the Lord. He always prefaced it with saying that of course, he was only speaking vaguely--having never been himself, but it certainly would be worth any and every suffering on earth. That was indisputable.

Penelope remembered specifics of her reverend's depictions like how all her friends and family that had passed would be there--pets, as well. There would be no such thing as being "tired" or "irritable" or "moody"--it would be warm elation at all times. The Lord's presence would be unlike anything they had ever felt on earth. It would surpass one's first kiss, one's wedding, the birth of one's children, one's children's weddings, anything. All would pale in comparison to the joys and comforts of True Paradise.

What a goddamn liar.

It was bad enough they had to die together, but Penelope quickly learned that specifically because they passed under the same circumstance, they had forged some sort of cosmic connection, which she could only pray would not extend for all eternity.

Denny led the way as they began to explore what he shrewdly referred to as "Juiced Up Disney World". It seemed that there were endless attractions that one could just embark upon any moment one liked. They were initially very reluctant to enter any of them, and it was actually GR who spurred them into the first. She screeched when she saw one that gave her a chance to see The Rolling Stones perform in concert, and not just any concert either... the 1969 Altamont Speedway performance, in fact.

Penelope had no clue, but the Altamont Free Concert was one of the most iconic moments in music history. Often referred to as "Woodstock West", the massive event saw over 300,000 people gather to see, among others: Santana, Jefferson Airplane, and of course, The Stones. Denny didn't know any of this either, but as soon as GR trotted those thigh high boots toward the entrance, he followed, so Penelope had no choice but to tail, as well.

As her boyfriend and the bimbo rocked out, Penelope couldn't help but think of a certain Rolling Stones' song about *sympathy* that would make it very much a conflict of interest for them to book a gig like this in heaven. Not to mention the whole premarital relations, drugs, and rock & roll thing. Watching the gap-toothed junkie that ended her life rock her head back and forth while simulating devil horns by pulling her middle and ring fingers down and letting her index and pinky rise, she started to wonder if there was a manager or something she could speak with, if for nothing else, just to get a better grip on what exactly was happening.

The thing was, outside of Matt--there were no angels, saintly types, ushers, or anything like that here. In fact, the people weren't even like... here. No one looked in her direction or made any kind of note of her presence, which she at first assumed was what heaven was because she hated being stared at or bothered when out in public, but now she needed literally anybody to give her some kind of insight. Well... anyone but these rock & roll heathens.

They ended the "night" by storming the stage and enduring Gaby*Rella dueting with that filthy man, Mick Jagger. Then the trio exited and looked for something else to do. Penelope grabbed Denny's hand and held it tight in hopes that her slower pace would drag him back as well. When she had created enough space between them and GR, she asked if maybe they should do something with just the two of them now (or just do that exclusively from now on). Denny replied that since time was not an issue here, that would be fine, and that was all Penelope needed to yank him in the other direction and roll into whatever the closest attraction was.

Penelope much preferred this one because it was so simple--nothing more than a slightly crowded ice rink. Now, she did not know how to skate, but as expected as soon as she hit the ice, she glided flawlessly around the facility. After a few laps just in the enjoyment of this new skill and its completely unearned sense of accomplishment, she skated back to Denny and once more grabbed his hand.

Denny asked her how she was liking heaven and after fighting the urge to shrug off her disappointment, she came clean and told him that it was really nothing like Rev. Cutter had described. Denny assured her that it was still new and they'd get the hang of it soon enough. Surely, she wasn't expecting trumpeting angels and people dressed in white robes and halos. Penelope decided it was best to not state that Denny's description was EXACTLY what she had expected.

Instead, she told him that as she hung upside down in the car, feeling her busted bones and punctured organs, and coming to terms with the fact that she was not going to walk away from this wreck... she was elated. Then when she saw that Denny was already well on his way to the Promised Land, she couldn't contain her smile despite the pain it cost to show it. She had gone to church every single Sunday, done the whole volunteer thing, and had made more than enough investments into the Jesus Bank to easily withdraw one ticket to heaven. On top of all of this, she wouldn't have to wait for the love of her life to join her because they were perishing simultaneously, which was something she had prayed for so, so much.

Yet, now... it seemed like all she was doing was third-wheeling, and she would be doing so indefinitely. Denny immediately shot down her worries and said that even if all three of them died together, it was the two of them who entered heaven hand-in-hand, just like they were right now. Though she did blush at his words, she was still unconvinced. She took a beat before slowly inquiring if he really thought this was all heaven was.

Before he could answer, Gaby*Rella skated up next to them--wearing a very low-cut crop top, because apparently ice didn't need to be cold in heaven. She butted in and spoke of how cool this was, just like it was in Milwaukee or something. Honestly, Penelope could barely understand her half the time because so much slang tainted her diction. (What kind of unholy act was "going HAM" exactly?) Before she could get a word in, GR challenged them to a three lap race and took off, naturally being tailed by Denny immediately.

Penelope half-assed her way around the rink until finally the two were coming up on her, threatening to put her a lap down. Her mind began to wander as she heard her lover and the overrated autotune machine laugh and tease as they came up full-speed behind her. Then as they got close enough, she heard a new voice. This one was so clear and succinct. In fact, it was her voice.

Turn around and trip the bitch. Maybe she'll die again and go somewhere else.

This, of course, was when she realized... she was definitely not in heaven.

Back when Penelope and Denny had only been dating for about six months--she still wouldn't even let him French her-- there was an innocent-ish moment that could probably be retroactively upgraded to traumatic now.

She had spent the early afternoon driving out to the nearest Edible Arrangement retailer to pick up his favorite indulgence: the one with the white chocolate bananas and the dark chocolate pineapple. This was no easy task because the storefront was way out of town. To be honest, she could have just made it herself or picked up a knockoff one at the local market, but Denny liked the Edible Arrangement one, so that's what he'd get. See, she was going so far out of her way because Denny had proven to be about the sweetest boyfriend she had ever had. After half a year of dating, he had proven courteous, thoughtful, and above all, very respectful. She knew well that in this day and age, it was hard to find a boy who would be content with holding hands and kissing cheeks to satisfy his desires for physical intimacy.

After picking up the treat, she then drove straight over to his house. With such a long drive, she began thinking to herself. She was just so impressed with Denny and how he was clearly a perfect fit to start grooming to become her husband. In fact, over the past few weeks, she had engaged in some careful consideration and Scriptural analysis, and it was at this very moment she decided that if it came up, she would allow him to fondle her breasts tonight, above the blouse of course, and if anything of his inflated, it would come to an immediate halt. She smiled ear to ear with thoughts of how happy her love would be to know the Arrangement was only the first treat that awaited him.

She wanted to surprise him, so she gave no prior notice. She parked down the block, made sure her boobs were presentable, then sent a heads-up text to his parents. When she arrived at the door, they opened it as silently as they could, and Penelope crept her way up the stairs toward Denny's room, nearly squealing with anticipation.

In any other circumstance, she would have of course knocked, but she was so giddy with excitement and the thrill of what he'd look like upon seeing his gorgeous girlfriend holding his absolute favorite treat that she quickly grabbed the knob and flung the door open in one rapid movement.

What she found was her beau with his hand cupping an old sock over his own "knob"... goofishly trying to shut off the Gaby*Rella music video playing on the screen.

After the rink, Denny said he wanted to find someplace with some sports to watch. Maybe they could even find Super Bowl I! Of course, Denny knew that GR was from Wisconsin and would also like the idea of seeing the Packers play and win such a memorable game. So, Penelope burst out into a rant about how much she hated football, which was a flat lie for the soul who could explain to a four-year-old when and how a Tampa Two defense should be implemented.

Penelope was so depressed that she missed the irony and horror of the fact that it was impossible to be so tired of a place where time didn't exist. Every attraction was the same. Something she hated, yet GR and Denny had such a blast. She almost wished he would just put his warm, soft hands all over her plastic chest and just fornicate with her already since that's obviously what they both wanted to do... for all eternity, it seemed. The limbo of it all was almost more taxing than the act itself.

Why was this happening to her? She had already confirmed that although Denny--with his pretty lit-up hazel eyes all over that whore--had reached Nirvana, she was in some kind of personalized hell. But why?

It was right at this moment that she saw Matt again. Not wanting to bring GR further into her business, she crept away from the two and boldly asked the child what the hell was going on--a poor choice of words, she realized in hindsight. He looked up at her with his disproportionately-sized eyes and told her she must know. She replied that she certainly did not. The child cracked a smile that pushed his plump cheeks up even chubbier and told her to start by thinking back to the crash.

She did her best to remember what she could have possibly done that night to deserve such a fate. However, truth be told, she didn't have many memories of that night, what with the two or three bottles of wine she had downed before Matthews and the Gang even hit the stage. From there... she remembered walking down that god-awful hill with Denny. He was holding her up and maybe she was singing--or was it yelling? Then there was the parking lot. Definitely yelling there, someone was checking out Denny, she assumed.

Why is she remembering being behind the wheel? It was Denny's car they took and she didn't drive that night... or did she?

And just like that, it all came back to her.

She remembered cursing at the people behind her after they politely asked that she consider not standing up during the entire performance. She also re-lived knocking the beer out of the woman's hand who accidentally bumped into her on the way to the ladies' room, then accused another stranger of touching Denny and trying to steal him from her.

It went on like this as she also recollected speaking exceedingly of the stench of some of the homeless people who showed up to the various charity events of her past. There were also the times when she flipped the sign CLOSED at the diner when there was still fifteen minutes left and she saw a family of --what she described as "troublemaking"--African Americans getting out of their car in hopes of a late dinner.

Finally, she got back to the moments before her death. She had hassled Denny to let her drive his car, despite an ungodly blood alcohol level. This included slapping him right across his cheek, then calling him a 'little bitch" when his eyes started to water. She managed to get onto the freeway, and after ranting about how those sluts at the Bowl have probably never been to church and will all burn in hell anyway, she swerved left into GR's Mercedes and brought them all here.

Back in Zion, she looked ahead at Denny and Gaby*Rella, and having been humbled by her own horrific actions, realized the pop star wasn't stealing her soulmate. They were just falling in love. He liked her because... behind the fake tits, the dyed blue hair, and the completely unbelievable mink eyelashes, she was actually a sweet and honest person. That's why she made heaven, and this proud Christian didn't.

Heaven really was everything Reverend Cutter had described. It's just that Penelope didn't fit in because she was closer to a demon than an angel. Heaven was the only place in existence where there was only the Truth, and the Truth was Denny deserved a partner like Gaby*Rella, GR deserved to see all these amazing concerts and experience events with a man as awesome as Denny, and Penelope didn't deserve shit. She had literally spent this entire spell actively trying to limit her boyfriend's paradise by pulling him away from who and what he really wanted. Obviously, it was not enough to make him spend his life with her unfulfilled, she wanted to deprive his eternity, as well.

Her steps slowed and the pair continued walking ahead, not missing their third wheel one bit. After a moment, they disappeared completely and Penelope was all alone. She stood still as the attractions started to fade around her and she became enveloped in empty space. She stared at her scuffed Keds and pondered the next move, but soon enough, she realized that there was no next move. She had failed. She died with sin on her--a lot of it.

With nothing left to do, she decided to sit. She crossed her legs and closed her eyes. Soon, more memories came back and she began to relive all of the infractions that her less enlightened self had undertaken, one by one, and she tried her best to focus on them intently so as to forget the fact that Denny and Gaby were probably holding hands right now.